He stared at the woman. "Taryn?"

Eyes that striking were hard to forget. Even though she'd been only a kid the last time he'd seen her.

"That's me." She shifted from one foot to the other, tucking her short, golden-brown hair behind her ear.

"Wow. I haven't seen you since you were what… twelve?"

She wrinkled her nose. "Try seventeen."

Way to go, Coble. "Sorry." He glanced at the tray in his hand. "Something sure smells good. This wouldn't be for Gramps, would it?"

"It is."

He couldn't help grinning. "Well, darlin', allow me to assist you then."

Her smile evaporated. "Suit yourself." Turning on her heel, she advanced up the wooden steps, leaving Cash to wonder if he'd offended her with the age remark.

"I thought I heard voices out here." Gramps held the storm door wide. "Smells like you've been baking again, young lady."

Pink tinged Taryn's cheeks. "It's almost Valentine's Day, Mr. Jenkins. Lots of people are baking."

Cash focused on the girl who had once followed him and her brother all over Ouray. "Beautiful and a great cook. That ought to make some man very happy one day."

Books by Mindy Obenhaus

Love Inspired

The Doctor's Family Reunion
Rescuing the Texan's Heart

MINDY OBENHAUS

always dreamed of being a wife and mother. Yet as her youngest of five children started kindergarten, a new dream emerged—to write stories of true love that would glorify God. Mindy grew up in Michigan, but got to Texas just as fast as she could. Nowadays she finds herself trapped in the city, longing for ranch life or the mountains. When she's not penning her latest romance, she likes cooking, reading, traveling and spending time with her grandkids. Learn more about her at www.mindyobenhaus.com.

Rescuing the Texan's Heart

Mindy Obenhaus

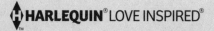

Recycling programs for this product may not exist in your area.

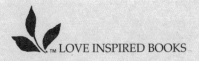 LOVE INSPIRED BOOKS

ISBN-13: 978-0-373-87912-0

RESCUING THE TEXAN'S HEART

Copyright © 2014 by Melinda Obenhaus

www.Harlequin.com

Printed in U.S.A.

The Lord brings death and makes alive.
—*1 Samuel* 2:6

To the men and women of Ouray Mountain Rescue Team

Acknowledgments

Becky Yauger, amazing writing partner and true friend.
Thanks for keeping me on task,
for seeing my warts and loving me anyway.

To my wonderful family, your love, support
and encouragement mean the world to me.
You inspire me to follow my dreams.

Many thanks to Ted and Betty Wolfe
and Brandy Ross for your friendship
and for helping me bring Ouray to life.

Chapter One

He didn't want to be here.

Eyeing the snow-laden peaks that spread in every direction, Cash Coble tightened his grip on the steering wheel of his rented SUV and slowly navigated the hairpin turns leading into Ouray. He'd reeled in two new dealers over the past two weeks and, thanks to a new manufacturing plant, business at Coble Trailers showed no signs of slowing down.

Meaning, Cash couldn't afford to, either.

I's had to be dotted. T's needed to be crossed. In Cash's world, there was no such thing as a relaxing weekend.

It's only three days.

He took a deep breath, mentally chastising himself for being so selfish. Gramps had never been too busy when it came to Cash. So why couldn't he show the old man the same courtesy?

A sharp right curve on the Million Dollar Highway and Cash glimpsed the town that he'd once hoped to call home. Nestled in a bowl among southwestern Colorado's majestic San Juan Mountains, Ouray was like no place else. Gramps always said it was heaven on earth. And, after all these years, Cash still agreed.

So why had it been so long since his last visit?

He sighed, rubbing the back of his neck.

Work. Work that was in Dallas, not Ouray.

No point in dwelling on what could never be.

But you're here now.

Only because his mother was caring for his two-year-old niece while his very pregnant sister was sentenced to bed rest. Yet that didn't stop Mom from insisting Cash take her place. All because Gramps had been dealing with a little bronchitis. Of course, the man was ninety. And when Mom got insistent, neither Cash nor his dad stood a chance.

Clouds gave way to the early-afternoon sun illuminating the businesses that lined Main Street. The corners of his mouth twitched. The rows of colorful Victorian buildings still held the charm of a bygone era when miners and gold were the lifeblood of this town.

Two blocks and a couple of right turns later, Cash eased the SUV to a stop in front of his grandfather's house. The 1920s two-story didn't look quite the way he remembered. Peeling green paint and a roof that had seen better days made the house seem neglected. Forgotten.

Kind of like your grandfather.

The thought jarred him. Had it really been ten years since his last visit?

He shifted the vehicle into Park and pulled the key from the ignition. What happened to him? There was a time when he would have leaped at the opportunity to visit his grandfather. Now it had taken coercion.

Exiting the SUV, he sucked in a breath of the freshest air he'd smelled in ages and lingered over the view. Ouray was the antithesis of Dallas. The closest things to mountains there were made of metal and glass. Man's handiwork sure paled next to God's.

He unzipped his jacket, the temperature warmer than

he expected. Remnants of snow still clung to life in shady areas, while dirty mounds dwindled away on street corners. Not exactly what he'd hoped for. It was February, after all, and this was Colorado. There should be plenty of snow. Even an inch or two would appease his Texas heart.

"Scout…stop that." Somewhere behind him, a female giggled.

Turning, he glimpsed a young woman crossing the patch of brown grass that was Gramp's side yard. She held a foil-covered tray in each hand, while a small wire-haired pup playfully nipped at her shoes.

"Scout! You're going to make me fall."

The dog all but ignored the hint of reprimand in the woman's tone and continued to dart in and around her feet.

That is, until it spotted Cash. The animal jerked to a halt.

Unaware, the woman stumbled over the dog, sending one of the platters airborne.

Ignoring the ache in his left knee from sitting too long, Cash rushed up the walk, intercepting the tray before it reached the ground.

The startled dog let out a high-pitched bark and lunged toward him.

The woman straightened. "Scout! No!"

Hoping to maintain an air of composure, Cash eased onto his good knee and held out his free hand. "Scout, is it?" He kept his voice gentle. "Well, hello there."

The pint-size mixed breed sniffed his fist. Its ears went back and tail wagged.

Cash couldn't help smiling. He missed having a dog. Life just hadn't been the same since Mickey died last year.

"There you go." He stroked the animal's sandy-colored fur. "See, I'm not so bad."

Standing, he met the woman's gaze.

"Sorry about that, Cash." Her pale blue eyes were unusually stunning. Especially against her tanned skin. The kind that could knock a guy right off his feet. She smiled. "Your grandfather said you were coming. Matter of fact, he hasn't talked about anything else."

The knife of guilt twisted.

He stared at the woman. "Taryn?" Eyes that striking were hard to forget. Even though she was only a kid the last time he'd seen her.

"That's me." She shifted from one foot to the other, tucking her short, golden-brown hair behind her ear.

"Wow. I haven't seen you since you were what... twelve?"

She wrinkled her nose. "Try seventeen."

Way to go, Coble. "Sorry." He glanced at the tray in his hand. "Something sure smells good. This wouldn't be for Gramps, would it?"

"It is."

He couldn't help grinning. "Well, darlin', allow me to assist you then."

Her smile evaporated. She stiffened. "Suit yourself." Turning on the heel of her rubber-soled shoes, she advanced up the wooden steps, leaving Cash to wonder if he'd offended her with the age remark.

Women. He'd never understand them.

He followed her, noting the large supply of wood stacked at one end of the porch. Surely Gramps hadn't cut all that himself.

Taryn reached past the handle of a snow shovel for the bell, when the door opened.

"I thought I heard voices out here." Gramps held the storm door wide. His white hair was as thick as ever and his green eyes brightened when he caught sight of Cash. "Come in. Come in."

If first impressions meant anything, Cash's mother was worried for nothing. The old man looked great.

Scout trotted inside first, as though she belonged, followed by Taryn and Cash.

The old house looked much better on the inside. The dark wood paneling in the living and formal dining space had been painted white, brightening the room considerably. Looked like Gramps had a new recliner, too. Seemed he wore one out about every five years or so. The floral sofa, though, still looked as new as the day Cash's grandmother bought it.

"I thought you'd be at the ice park." Gramps smiled at Taryn.

"No, not today."

The old man shifted his attention back to Cash, his chest puffed out. "Did you know that Ouray is the ice climbing capital of America?"

"I did not." However, he couldn't help noticing that the console TV was still parked near the front window so it could be viewed from the kitchen.

"We even have a big ice festival. But that was last month."

Cash always said his grandfather should be a spokesperson for the town. The old man never missed an opportunity to talk up Ouray.

"Pretty nice setup they've got over there, though." Gramps inhaled deeply. "Smells like you've been baking again, young lady."

Pink tinged Taryn's cheeks. "It's almost Valentine's Day, Mr. Jenkins. Lots of people are baking."

"So what's your excuse the rest of the year?" The old man looked at Cash. "This sweet thing keeps me on baked goods that rival anything your grandmother would have made."

Cash focused on the girl who had once followed him and her brother all over Ouray. "Beautiful *and* a great cook. That ought to make some man very happy."

Those clear blue eyes narrowed for a split second.

"I'll take this." She snatched the tray from his hand and headed into the kitchen.

He turned to his grandfather. He hadn't seen the old man since the last time he'd come to Texas, shortly after the birth of Cash's niece. That was over two years ago. And while one would never guess the man to be ninety, the telltale signs of age had grown more numerous. Lines revealed a man who loved the outdoors and age spots dotted his tanned skin.

"How are you, Gramps?"

His grandfather drew him into a warm embrace. "Even better now, son." He clapped Cash on the back with a strength that belied his age. "I can't tell you how good it is to see you again."

Funny how he had to stoop to hug this man he once considered a giant. He still smelled of coffee and outdoors. Home.

His grandfather released him.

"And the bronchitis?"

"Oh, I'm fine. Taryn there nursed me back to health with her homemade chicken soup."

"Good." He looked around the familiar space where he'd spent so much of his childhood. "It's good to be here. Thank you for inviting me."

Gramps sent him a stern look. "No invitation needed. You know you're always welcome."

The moisture in the old man's eyes tugged at Cash's heart. Suddenly, he was glad he'd come. A few days in Ouray might do wonders for him. Who knows? He might even relax. Clear his head. And, with any luck, see a little snow.

* * *

First, *darlin',* then *beautiful.*

Taryn Purcell had heard those words before. And they made her skin crawl worse than nails on a chalkboard.

It took all the restraint she could muster not to dump the cherry pie and other goodies she'd made onto Art Jenkins's kitchen table. She loved the old man as much as her own grandfather, but his grandson left much to be desired.

She huffed out a sigh. Cash Coble. A big name for a big man with an even bigger ego, no doubt. Was it just her or were all tall, good-looking Texans arrogant and condescending? Like a woman's sole purpose was to cook and look good for her man.

That's probably how Cash preferred his women—in the kitchen, barefoot and pregnant.

Hmph. Bet Big Tex wouldn't have the guts to strap on some crampons, grab an ax and scale some fat ice. Boy, she'd like to teach him a thing or two.

"Taryn…" Mr. Jenkins's voice drew closer.

She turned as he entered the kitchen with his grandson. From his short blond hair to his boot-cut jeans and pointy cowboy boots, Cash had Texan written all over him. Right down to the swagger. And those dimples…

Biting her lip, she shifted her attention to Scout, who was happily tucked under Cash's arm, licking him as if the man was a side of beef. Scout was usually afraid of men. Even Mr. Jenkins had to bribe her with a treat before the mutt allowed him to pick her up. And he'd known her since she was a puppy.

"You remember my grandson, Cash, don't you?"

She gripped the metal edge of the ancient Formica-topped table behind her and forced a smile. "I do. Not that we spent much time together." Cash was five years older than her, the same age as her brother Randy. Guess that would make him thirty-two.

Mischief glinted in Cash's green eyes. "No, but I sure remember how you used to spy on Randy and me."

She squared her shoulders. "I was *not* spying."

"Aw, come on. Every time I turned around I'd see you ducking behind something."

He saw me?

She lifted her chin, her trail shoes scraping across the worn gold-and-orange sheet vinyl. "Well, somebody had to make sure you two stayed out of trouble."

Turning her attention back to his grandfather, she said, "There's a cherry pie—" she pointed to the foil-wrapped pastry "—and then here we have some banana nut bread, chocolate chip cookies and brownies."

The old man gave her a one-armed hug. "You sure know how to spoil a fella."

She kissed his weathered cheek. "Some people are simply worth spoiling." Stepping back, her gaze inadvertently fell to Cash. True, she'd brought enough baked goods for two, though she never imagined she would actually run into Cash.

Her heart skittered to a halt. *Oh, no.* He probably thought she was waiting for him to pull up before she brought this stuff over.

Talk about lousy timing.

"I...need to get back to the house." She retrieved her Chihuahua-terrier mix from Cash's muscular arms and hurried through the living room as if she had something burning in the oven. But she had to get out of here before she said or did something she'd regret.

"Thank you, again," Mr. Jenkins called behind her as she opened the door.

"You're welcome." She squeezed Scout tighter and continued onto the porch and down the steps, feeling as though someone had sucked the air out of her lungs.

Clouds covered the sun as she hurried to the Victorian

house next door. She could only imagine what was going through Cash's mind. Everyone knew what a huge crush she'd had on him as a kid. And seeing him now, that same sensation had wriggled through her once again. Then he called her darlin'.

She stomped up the back steps. That single word was like a splash of icy water. The last time she fell for that line it had cost her far more than anyone knew.

She nuzzled Scout's wiry fur. "Can I get some sugar?" Some people thought her crazy for talking to her dog like a baby. But her brothers' opinions weren't of any concern to her. Besides, Scout was her baby and Taryn loved her every bit as much as her brothers loved their kids.

Scout licked her nose.

"Thank you."

Inside her parents' kitchen, she set Scout on the wooden floor and shrugged out of her fleece vest. Cash still looked as amazing as she remembered. The only thing that had changed was that the good-looking boy had grown into a fine-looking man. The kind that knew how to make a woman feel special. Loved.

That is, until he was finished with her.

Like Brian.

Gooseflesh prickled down her arms.

I'm not totally heartless, darlin'.

She tossed her vest over a hook near the door, slumped into one of six straight-back chairs surrounding the oak table and rubbed the chill away.

If only her shame were so easy to erase.

Cool air infiltrated the room as her mother, Bonnie Purcell, swept through the door with several grocery sacks.

Taryn shoved to her feet. "Let me help you, Mom."

"Oh, thank you, honey."

She took the bags, settled them on the granite countertop—her mom's big splurge when she had the kitchen remodeled last spring—and unloaded the items while her mother removed her jacket.

"I see there's an SUV parked in front of Art's house. I wonder if Cash has arrived."

Scout's nails clicked against the hand-scraped oak as she trotted across the kitchen to dance at her mom's feet.

Taryn focused on emptying the bags. If she let on that she'd been next door, her mother would home in on that and assume Taryn still had a crush on Cash.

Her mom scooped up the dog, continuing toward Taryn and staring next door.

She followed her mother's gaze. "Uh, yeah. I saw him go inside." Not a lie, just not full disclosure.

"I bet Art is tickled to death." Her mother turned her way, brushing her dark brown bangs to one side. "That boy has always held such a special place in his heart. I think he really believed Cash would end up in Ouray one day."

"Didn't he take over his father's company or something?" Trying to act nonchalant, Taryn dumped a fresh bag of flour into the large glass canister on the counter.

"I don't think he took it over, just stepped in to run things when his father got sick."

Taryn had been too wrapped up in herself back then to remember what happened. "Sick how?"

"Cancer."

She dared to meet her mother's gaze. "Is he okay?"

"Oh, yes." Her mom set Scout to the floor. "But it was touch and go for a while. They make livestock trailers, you know. Cattle, horses…." She wadded up the empty grocery bags and tucked them in the pantry. "From what I hear, the company has really grown with Cash at the helm. There aren't many young men who would give up their own dreams to step in and help their father like that."

Once again, Taryn's gaze trailed to the house next door. Perhaps. But she knew all too well that a guy could live up to his family's expectations and still be a heel. Her heart had the scars to prove it.

Turning, she concentrated on the rest of the groceries. Yep, the best thing she could do was steer clear of Cash Coble. Because no matter how enticing it might be to revisit childhood dreams, Cash was a heartbreak waiting to happen. And she had no intention of going through that ever again.

"I can hardly wait to see him," her mother gushed. "Which is why I went ahead and invited them for dinner."

Taryn halted, terror clipping through her veins. "Dinner? Tonight?"

"Why, yes. We agreed to move our family dinner to tonight since you'll be at Blakely's wedding rehearsal tomorrow."

"I know that, but Cash isn't family."

"He's just like family. And he's only in town for a few days. Besides—" Her mother grabbed a package of toilet paper. Matchmaking mirth glinted in her gray-blue eyes as she started out of the room. "I hear he's still single."

Taryn cringed. "Mom, *please* don't go there." The last thing Taryn needed was a man. What she did need, however, was a life. Some semblance of a future. Twenty-seven years old and she still lived with her parents. How was that for pathetic?

Sure, she loved climbing and teaching people to overcome their fears, but she couldn't live at home forever. She needed something to call her own. And since this morning's chat with Mr. Ramsey at All Geared Up, Ouray's one-stop shop for outdoor enthusiasts, she just might have a plan.

But first she had to make it through dinner.

Chapter Two

Cash let the cream-colored sheer curtain fall back into place and turned away from the window that overlooked the yard between Gramps's house and the Purcells'. He still couldn't shake the feeling that he'd said or done something to offend Taryn. But, for the life of him, he couldn't figure out what.

She'd seemed so friendly initially. Then, suddenly, it was as if he'd slapped her. The hurt in those incredible blue eyes right before she charged out of the house had bothered him ever since.

"How about some pie?" Gramps called from the kitchen.

Cash shook his head, willing the crazy thoughts out of his mind. "Sure." He bypassed the antique drop-leaf table that had been tucked against the dining room wall and joined his grandfather.

Taking a seat in one of the four green vinyl chairs, he pulled out his phone. "You have internet, Gramps?"

"Inter-what?"

"Internet. You know, the World Wide Web, computers…"

"No, sir." Standing at the narrow strip of faux butcher-block counter between the refrigerator and the sink, the old man deposited a heaping mound of pie onto a plate. "Don't intend to, either."

Seriously? How could anyone live without the internet? Then again, this was Gramps.

Cash mentally kicked himself for not buying one of those mobile hot-spot devices that allowed him to connect to the internet anywhere. For now, he'd have to rely on his smart phone for email. But first thing tomorrow, he and his laptop would be tracking down the nearest Wi-Fi connection so he could get some work done.

He tapped the mail icon and waited for the page to load. Since he'd turned off the volume, it vibrated in his hand, indicating he had mail.

He scrolled to the top of the page. A distributor wanted a quote.

"Here you go." Gramps set a loaded plate in front of him, along with a fork.

"Thanks." Maybe Cash could calculate the quote later this evening and email it via his phone. That way, the customer would have it by morning.

The next message was from his sister.

Subject : Have a good time.
Enjoy your time in Ouray, big brother. You have no idea how jealous I am, but the doctor refuses to let me travel. Just as well. I feel like a beached whale. I still can't believe I'm having twins.
Hug Gramps for me and give him my love.

Cash smiled. Prepregnancy, his little sister didn't weigh a hundred pounds soaking wet. Now, based on the pictures his mother had shown him, she looked as if she'd swallowed a blimp.

Gramps took a seat across from him.

"Megan sends her love."

The old man looked confused. "When did you talk to your sister?"

"Just now." He turned the screen so his grandfather could see. "She sent me an email."

"You gonna stare at that contraption the whole time you're here?" Gramps pointed with his fork. "Folks seem practically glued to those things these days."

"They do make staying in touch a lot easier. Email, text messaging—"

"What about a good old-fashioned phone call?"

Cash cleared his throat, fearful the comment had been directed at him. "They can do that, too. Hey, maybe we can FaceTime with Megan while I'm here. You'd be able to see her while you're talking to her."

The old man's bushy white brows shot up. "Is that a fact?"

"Yes, sir." Cash tucked his phone away, eyeing the fruit-filled pastry on his plate. "So, I take it Taryn does a lot of baking for you."

Gramps swallowed his first bite. "She bakes for everybody. Says it's therapeutic."

"In that case—" Cash lifted his loaded fork "—I'm all for therapy." The sweet, tart flavors burst onto his tongue. "Mmm… This is good." He stabbed another bite. "Forgive me for saying this, but didn't she used to be kind of a brat?"

His grandfather chuckled. "Taryn was a little too big for her britches, all right."

"I recall her brothers complaining that she always got her way."

"Well, she is the only girl." Gramps rested his fork on his plate. "And a pretty one, at that. In case you hadn't noticed."

"Oh, I noticed." A guy would have to be dead not to.

"Didn't I hear something about her leaving Ouray for a while?"

Nodding, Gramps cut another bite of pie with his fork. "Took off for college while the ink was still drying on her high school diploma."

Cash grabbed a napkin from the owl-shaped holder on the table. Wiped his mouth. "Where'd she go?"

"Texas."

"No kidding."

"Finished her first semester, then told her folks she was taking some time off to think about what she wanted to do with her life."

Cash hiked up the sleeves of his Henley a notch and grabbed another forkful. "That's not unusual. Lots of kids get confused once they get to college."

"I suppose." Gramps studied his pie as if looking for answers. "'Cept Phil and Bonnie never knew where she was. About worried themselves sick."

"You mean, she didn't stay in touch?"

He shrugged. "On occasion. But anytime they offered to come see her or send money, she'd refuse."

Cash immediately thought of the drugs so often prevalent in college towns. Then again, most druggies wouldn't turn down a handout. They'd simply put it toward their next fix.

"Then one day, out of the blue, Taryn showed up back here." Gramps shook his head. "Never said a word about what went on. Just that Ouray was where she belonged."

"How long was she gone?"

The old man shrugged, going after another bite. "A year or so."

That left a big gap of time. "And you don't have any idea what happened to her?"

"None. And I don't think her parents do, either." Gramps pushed his half-empty plate aside then leaned forward, resting his arms on the table. His gaze bore into Cash. "But I do know that Taryn is no longer the self-absorbed girl we all remember. She's a Godly woman." Leaning back, he picked up his fork again. "One of the best mountain guides in town, too."

"Mountain guide?"

"Hiking, rock climbing, ice climbing…" He wagged his fork through the air. "That's her forte, you know."

Cash absently rubbed his knee. All things he'd never be able to enjoy again.

Gramps scooped up another bite of pie. "She's also on the Mountain Rescue Team."

"What's that?"

"A search and rescue team trained for our unique setting." The old man grinned. "I even had the privilege of joining them on a mission last summer. One of our local boys fell into Chief Ouray Mine."

Cash smiled at the old miner. "Let me guess, you had to navigate them through the mine?"

"Didn't know that going out, but I went along, just in case."

"Was the kid okay?" Cash finished his pie.

"A few scrapes and bruises."

He picked up his empty plate and started toward the sink. "Sounds like Taryn's an integral part of the community." Which made him wonder why she had been so eager to leave in the first place. She'd obviously decided the big city wasn't all glitz and glamour. But why had she stayed away so long?

Rinsing the dish, he contemplated his interaction with her. The way she seemed to bristle every time he said something that would flatter most women. And he wanted to know why.

Considering he was only in Ouray for a few days, un-raveling the mystery of the girl next door seemed nearly impossible. Then again, it wasn't like him to back down from a challenge. Especially one as intriguing as Taryn Purcell.

"Maybe that'll give you two something to discuss tonight."

He jerked his head toward his grandfather. "What's tonight?"

"Bonnie and Phil Purcell invited us for dinner. Apparently the whole family is looking forward to seeing you."

A gust of wind rattled the windows, drawing their attention outside.

"Looks like that front's finally arrived." Gramps stood with his plate. "Things are s'posed to turn mighty chilly."

Given Taryn's abrupt exit, Cash was certain of it.

Taryn paused at the front door, her hand on the antique bronze knob, while Scout barked behind her.

Cash is not Brian. And he is not *interested in you.* He's a family friend. Just like his grandfather. Though considerably more handsome.

He called you darlin'.

She squeezed her eyes shut. *Lord, please help me to be kind to Cash. I realize he did nothing wrong. That it's my past with Brian that is causing me to behave so horribly.*

"Are you going to open it, or let our guests freeze to death on the front porch?" Her big brother, Randy, stared down at her.

Since when did he pull himself away from the sports channel for anything but food?

"I'm warning you, Randy. If you say one thing to embarrass me…"

"Nah. I'll leave that to Mom." He nudged Taryn away from the door and turned the knob. "By the way, you look really nice tonight."

Peering down at the soft blue, ultrafeminine sweater,

she wished she'd gone with the bulky cable knit. She glared back at Randy with half a mind to wallop him. But their mother would never stand for it. After all, appearances were everything in Bonnie Purcell's world.

Instead, Taryn picked up her dog, leaving her big brother to do the honors of greeting their guests while she made her way to the kitchen to help her mother and her sister-in-law, Amanda.

At least she'd bought herself a little time before she had to face Cash again. Strange to think that there was a time when she wouldn't have felt the least bit guilty for treating someone so ugly. But she wasn't that person anymore. And God had been prodding her all afternoon, letting her know what He required of her.

Still, she didn't have to apologize in front of everyone. She'd wait for just the right opportunity. Even if it took all night.

"Yes. Absolutely you need to meet Cash." Taryn's mother motioned for Randy's wife to follow and nearly plowed into Taryn at the kitchen door. "Where are you going?"

"The kitchen?"

Her mother whirled her back around. "Not until you've greeted our guests, you don't. Now, go." She all but shoved Taryn across the wooden flooring in the foyer.

Taryn hugged Scout a little closer. *And so it begins.*

"My goodness, Cash…" Her mom's arms went wide as she approached. "It's so good to see you again."

Taryn kind of felt sorry for the guy when her mother embraced him like a long-lost son. She had to hand it to him, though. Cash didn't look the least bit taken aback by the welcome. "It's nice to be here. Thank you for inviting me."

"Nonsense." Her mom released him. "You're like family."

"How's it going, Cash?" Her father stepped forward to shake his hand.

"Just fine, sir. Thank you."

"There's Gage," her mom continued.

Taryn's second brother waved from the adjacent living room, then gestured to the four-year-old in his arms. "This is my daughter, Emma, and—" he pointed to the golden-haired girl who had already latched onto Mr. Jenkins's hand "—that's Cassidy over there."

Cash acknowledged them with a smile and a nod. "Girls."

Randy snagged Amanda around the waist and inched her closer. "This is my wife, Amanda."

"It's nice to finally meet you." She held out her hand. "I've heard a lot about you."

Cash took hold. "All good, I hope."

"For the most part." Amanda and Randy exchanged a playful, loving glance. One that always made Taryn wonder if there was someone in this world who could love her like that. Completely and unconditionally. As though she was the only one who mattered.

"This is our son, Steven." Randy hoisted the five-year-old into his arms.

"Hey there, champ." Cash held up a high-five and Taryn's nephew smacked it.

Everyone laughed, drowning out the basketball action blaring from the fifty-inch flat-screen in the living room.

Her mom grabbed Cash's arm, turning him ever so slightly. "And here's our little Taryn, all grown up."

Everyone standing in front of her parted like the Red Sea, adding to her mortification.

Repeatedly stroking Scout's wiry fur, she fought the urge to run screaming from the room as all eyes shifted to her. Including Cash's.

His knee-buckling smile made it impossible to move, though. "Yes, we met earlier."

Heat singed her cheeks, a rare occurrence for someone with her olive complexion. Still, she would bet that her cheeks were as red as the cherry jelly beans she'd bought to give to her nieces and nephew on Valentine's Day.

"Oh…?" Interest sparked in her mother's eyes. No way the woman with a penchant for matchmaking was letting that one sail by unnoticed.

"She brought some desserts over for Gramps. Which—" his attention shifted back to Taryn "—were *really* good."

Mr. Jenkins cleared his throat. "Speaking of food, it sure smells good in here." He shot Taryn a stealthy wink. At least someone had her back.

"Taryn makes the best stew you've ever tasted," her mom boasted. "And her rolls are positively to die for."

"Wait till you see the table decorations." Desperate to shift the spotlight to someone else, Taryn continued, "Mom really outdid herself."

Her mother half-heartedly waved off the compliment. "Oh, I just threw a few odds and ends together, that's all." Her gaze flitted to the dining room on the other side of the foyer. "But it did turn out quite nice."

"Sounds like the Purcell women are a talented lot." Cash's gaze settled on Taryn, sending another wave of heat surging up her neck.

Unfortunately, she had not inherited her mother's flair for decorating. She could probably manage a decent grouping of candles, but her mom knew how to make things look perfect.

"You simply find a way to cover up the flaws," she always said.

Nuzzling a squirming Scout, Taryn thought about all the flaws in her life. The ones she'd worked so hard to cover up since returning to Ouray. Perhaps she was more like her mother than she thought. She had more scrapes and scars than the old hutch that was the focal point of Mom's new kitchen.

She set the wiggling pup on the floor, wishing she, too, could escape.

"Phil, why don't you take their coats while I get our guests something to drink." Her mother's attention shifted between Cash and his grandfather. "How about some hot spiced cider?"

"Cider sounds great, Mrs. Purcell."

"There's no need to be so formal, Cash. Call me Bonnie."

"A hot drink would be just dandy." Mr. Jenkins handed his jacket to her dad.

Six-year-old Cassidy caught her grandmother by the arm. "Nana, can you help me find the checkers so I can play with Mr. Jenkins?"

Her mom cupped Cassidy's chin. "You bet, punkin'."

Watching the tender exchange, Taryn couldn't help wondering if her mom would have accepted—

She shook her head. No, her mother had made it perfectly clear.

No daughter of mine will have a child out of wedlock. If you ever do that to me, I'll disown you.

Taryn understood, though. After all, her mother grew up as the illegitimate child of a scarlet woman. The last thing she wanted was to be the talk of the town.

"Taryn, honey—" her mother's voice jerked her from her thoughts "—would you be a dear and get those refreshments while I help Cassidy?"

What? And hide from inquiring minds?

"Two ciders coming up." The aroma of fresh-baked rolls made her stomach growl as she drew closer to the kitchen. She washed her hands then grabbed two mugs from the refurbished hutch, recalling how decrepit and unsightly the piece had been when her mother found it on somebody's curb. Actually, it wasn't even a hutch. More like someone's old pie safe. But with some new glass and a couple coats of red paint...

Yep, Bonnie Purcell knew how to dress things up, no matter how battered and beyond help they seemed to the untrained eye.

But Taryn wasn't a piece of furniture. She clutched the mugs to her chest and crossed the kitchen. If her mother ever learned the ugly truth of Taryn's time in Texas, she'd be deemed unsalvageable. Which is why no one could ever know.

Lifting the lid on the pot of mulled cider, she savored the scent of cinnamon and cloves before ladling the steaming drink into the mugs.

"It smells great in here." At the sound of Cash's voice, she jumped, sending the metal ladle crashing to the floor. "Whoa. Hey. I'm sorry." He knelt beside her to retrieve the utensil. "I didn't mean to startle you."

She set the lid back into place, determined to regain her wits before looking at him. Though the woodsy scent of his cologne wasn't doing much to help.

"I'm all right." Retrieving the dish towel from the counter beside the stove, she wiped a drip from the first cup before handing it to him. "And if anyone needs to say they're sorry, it's me." She took the ladle from him and dared to meet his puzzled gaze.

"You? Why?"

"I wasn't the friendliest person earlier today." She glanced past him to make sure no one else was coming. In particular, her mother, who would, no doubt, misconstrue their being alone in the same room.

"Taryn, I've met plenty of unfriendly people in my time and you are not one of them. A little flustered maybe."

Flustered? He thought she was flustered?

"That's what I get for teasing you, I suppose."

"Teasing?" She dropped the towel on the counter, rinsed the ladle in the sink.

"About you following me and Randy around." He sipped his drink. "Mmm. This ought to warm me up. It's freezing out there."

Her brain quickly retraced their earlier conversation. How stupid could she be?

She set the ladle beside the stove. Of course Cash was teasing her. Just like he used to do when she was a kid. Just like her brothers still do. She'd just been so tuned in to what she interpreted as smarmy to realize the difference.

And now that she did, she wasn't sure which was worse. The smooth-talking Cash or the Cash that still thought of her as a child.

Chapter Three

When the kids announced that it was snowing, Cash wanted to push away from Bonnie's dining room table and hurry outside to enjoy the sight. After all, in Dallas, snow rarely lasted more than a few minutes. Good thing he remembered he was a grown-up, though. Otherwise, his hosts might have thought him a little crazy.

Nonetheless, he was pleased to see the white flakes still falling in the darkness when he and Gramps bid the Purcells farewell.

"Phil and Bonnie have done an impressive job of restoring that old home." Cash glanced back at the gray Victorian. "That has to be some of the finest, most intricate millwork I've ever seen."

"They done good, all right." Despite the short walk, Gramps tugged on his nubby stocking cap and gloves. "Bonnie loves that sort of stuff." He nudged Cash with his elbow. "I see you quit picking the celery out of your stew."

Cash couldn't help laughing. "It took me a while, but I finally got used to it. Just don't expect me to eat it raw."

"So noted." The old man patted his now-protruding belly. "Yes, sir, that was one mighty fine meal."

"You'll get no argument from me. I can't tell you the

last time I ate that well." He rubbed his own stomach, suddenly regretting that third roll. "Or that much."

Gramps chuckled.

"By the way, thanks for giving me a heads-up on Gage's wife." His grandfather had shared how she'd taken off last year, leaving Gage to raise their two daughters alone. "The last thing I would have wanted was to create an awkward situation."

"Which is exactly why I told you." The old man started toward the back of the house.

"If you don't mind—" Cash paused in the side yard "—I think I'll stay out here for a bit and enjoy the snow." Not to mention check email without the fear of reprimand.

"Suit yourself. I'll be inside where it's warm."

"I won't be long." Especially since his "warm" coat didn't seem quite as warm here as it did in Dallas. At least the wind had died down.

He pulled out his phone and aimed the camera at a streetlight in a way that highlighted the falling snow. Satisfied with the shot, he forwarded it to his sister. That ought to make her jealous.

Leaning against the side of the house, he checked his email.

"Delayed shipment?" But Wiseman's was their largest distributor in Oklahoma. *How could we—?*

A high-pitched bark made him jerk his head up.

Taryn gasped and yanked on Scout's leash. "Cash! You scared me half to death. What are you doing lurking in the shadows like that?"

"Sorry." He held up his phone. "Just trying to get a little work done."

"Work, huh?" Her gaze narrowed. "Aren't you supposed to be on vacation?" She tried to shorten Scout's leash, but the pup squirmed toward him anyway, tail wagging frantically.

"Not exactly." He pocketed the phone and stooped to pet the dog. "You know what they say, no rest for the weary."

"They also say all work and no play makes Cash a dull boy."

Ouch! He glanced up at the feisty woman. Yvette had turned down his proposal with those same words.

"Come on." She tugged on the leash, started to walk away, then stopped and looked back at him. "Well, are you coming?"

"Me?" Standing, he fingered his chest.

"Yes, you. If you're going to be out in this cold, you need to keep moving."

Man, this girl didn't pull any punches. And for some odd reason, he kind of liked it.

He fell in line beside her, surreptitiously watching her every move. Taryn wasn't like any of the women he knew. They only seemed to care about clothes, shoes and how they looked. Taryn was gorgeous without even trying. And, from what he could tell, she cared about helping others.

As they walked, he burrowed his fists deeper into his poor excuse for a jacket, wishing he'd thought to grab his gloves. "I was hoping to see some snow. Think we'll get much?"

A few flakes clung to Taryn's purple beanie. Another item he'd failed to consider. "Nah. But don't worry. Winter's not over yet."

He cut her a sideways glance. "Easy for you to say. I leave on Sunday."

The corners of her mouth lifted. "You might be in luck then. There's more snow forecast for Saturday."

Scout trotted ahead of them as they wandered onto Third Avenue.

"It's so quiet here."

"For the most part." Her puffy white jacket made a

swishing sound as she swung her arms. "So how are things in the cattle trailer business?"

"Booming. At least for us."

"Those must be some special trailers." She let out some length on Scout's leash.

"Weight is our best selling point. We have the lightest empty weight in the business."

"And your dad designs them?"

"Yep. The whole thing's been his dream from the beginning."

They stopped while Scout took care of some business.

Taryn stared at him. "And what about you? Is it *your* dream?"

To say he was taken aback by her question would be an understatement. No one had asked about his dreams in a long time. Not since they were put on ice. Now the best he could hope for was to make his father proud.

He shrugged. "Like I said, business is booming."

She looked as though she could see right through him. But didn't say a word.

They started walking again.

By the time they turned onto Fourth Street, Cash was eager to change the subject and get some answers of his own. "Gramps tells me you're one of the best mountain guides in town."

She laughed. "Your grandfather is a bit biased, but I can hold my own."

They ducked under a limb that bowed over the sidewalk, while Scout tugged on her leash, nose to the ground.

"Climbing is in my blood. Though it wasn't until I came back to Ouray that I realized how important it was to me."

"Came back from where?"

"Texas."

"Really? Whereabouts?"

"I spent some time at UNT."

"University of North Texas. I know it well. Matter of fact, my brother-in-law went to school there. What was your major?"

"I wasn't there long enough to think about a major."

"So why'd you leave?" If she could apply the pressure, so could he.

"People change." For a moment, her expression clouded. Then she cleared her throat. "Besides, I missed the mountains."

"You ever thought about coming back to Texas? Maybe for a visit?"

Her exhaled breath clouded in the chilly night air. "Nope. Ouray is where I belong. It's a part of me, like climbing. Tackling a mountain or a massive slab of ice changes my perspective. I look back and see the path I took. A path that wasn't perfect. One that was steep and maybe a little slippery. But I made it." She looked at him now. "That empowers me."

He couldn't help wondering if she was talking more about climbing or life. But the passion that sparkled in her eyes drew him like the stars to the night. Had he ever been that passionate about anything?

"You certainly sold me."

In the glow of someone's porch light, her cheeks, already pink from the cold, deepened in color. "Then perhaps you should give it a try."

Taryn saw the excitement that brightened Cash's green eyes. Then fade just as quick. And despite telling herself repeatedly she was going to keep her distance, curiosity only drew her closer.

The heels of Cash's cowboy boots clipped along the sidewalk as they made their way down Fourth Street, their breath visible in the cool air.

"Did your grandfather ever take you climbing?"

Scout darted back and forth in front of them, searching for who knows what.

"Just hiking. I was always in awe of his connection to these mountains." Cash's gaze lifted. "He seemed to know everything about them. And never hesitated to share his passion. That man taught me geological, biological and theological lessons no one's ever heard in a classroom."

She laughed, having been on the receiving end of the old miner's passion a time or two herself. "Ever thought about giving ice climbing a try?"

"No. And I'm not sure I could." Resignation laced his tone.

"Why?"

"Bum knee. Tore a ligament my sophomore year of college."

"ACL?"

"You guessed it."

She grimaced. "What happened?"

"Me and some college buddies were goofing around on ATVs and I managed to flip mine."

"Did you have surgery?"

"Yeah. But the knee still bothers me every now and then."

"I see." Though glancing at his even stride, she didn't really. There were plenty of people with that same type of injury and they didn't seem to have any problems climbing. Just to be sure, though, she'd check with her friend Blakely's fiancé who also happened to be a doctor. "Do you work out?" As if she had to ask. She'd noticed the way his muscles strained the fabric of his shirt.

"I try to stay in shape."

"How's your core strength?"

"Not bad." The corners of his mouth twitched and she felt foolish for asking. "Why?"

"Climbing involves a lot of core strength."

He slowed. "I didn't know that."

"Well, now you do."

"Looks like it stopped snowing." Cash scanned the night sky and she wondered if he was trying to change the subject.

Still, she hadn't missed the disappointment in his voice. "For now."

He shivered. No wonder with that lightweight jacket. They'd best keep moving.

She picked up speed. "So what do you do in Dallas?"

He kicked at a rock as they walked. "I thought we discussed that already."

"I don't mean work. What do you do for fun?"

He shrugged, his hands still buried in his pockets. "I don't know. Hang out with friends. Watch football. I used to like taking my dog to the park, but since I don't have a dog anymore, well…seems kind of pointless."

She'd known he was a dog person from the moment he won Scout over. Brian had hated dogs. Not that it mattered.

"What kind of dog?"

"Siberian husky."

"Oooh…they're gorgeous."

"They are. And Mickey was a beaut. He could play fetch for hours. So much so that I usually wore out before he did."

She laughed. "So what happened to him?"

"Cancer. I had to have him put down last year." His excitement gone, he cleared his throat as though it had clogged with emotion.

She couldn't help it. She laid a hand on his arm, stopping him. "I'm sure that was very difficult."

"It was for the best." He hesitated to look at her.

"That doesn't make it any easier."

His gaze went to her hand first, then trailed to her face. Even in the dark, she saw a man who was struggling.

He looked…like a caged animal. Trapped somewhere he didn't want to be. Perhaps in a life he didn't want. From what she could gather, everything about Cash revolved around work. That wasn't living.

He started walking again, winding onto Fifth Avenue.

"Mickey would have loved Ouray." His focus was on the darkened mountaintops, but the wistfulness in his voice only added to her sense that Cash Coble was one unhappy man.

"And how does Mickey's owner feel about Ouray?"

"I used to dream of living here."

"So what happened?" She shortened Scout's leash to keep her close. "What kept you away for so long?"

"Obligations."

"What kind of obligations?" She knew she was being pushy but pressed anyway.

"Work. Family." He sounded winded. No doubt the altitude was getting to him, regardless of how fit he might be. After all, he started today at what, five thousand feet above sea level. Ouray sat at seventy-eight hundred.

"You have family here, too. Or does your grandfather fall in the obligation category?"

He jerked his head to look at her. "Are you trying to make me feel guilty?" His pained expression told her he did feel guilty.

Lord, I want to help him. Not make it worse.

"Not at all. Just curious what made you give up your dream." And why he was so sad.

"My father got sick." He kept walking, defensiveness lacing his tone. "I had to step in and run his company."

"But he's better now." *Shut up, Taryn. Let the poor man be.*

He stopped and glared at her. "My father built a business from the ground up. He poured his heart and soul into making it a success. Provided for us. Gave me, my sister and my mom the kind of life he never had. It means the world to him. You may not understand this, but I can't let him down."

Not understand? Boy, was that an understatement. And the reason no one but Blakely knew about David, the baby Taryn had given up for adoption.

She studied the man before her. The set of his jaw, the resigned slump of his shoulders told her this was something he had to do. No matter what it cost him.

"That's very admirable, Cash. But there's more to life than just work."

"Not in my father's world." He strode away.

She didn't know when she'd seen a person so miserable. Like Cash's only satisfaction in life, his identity, revolved around a job. A job he felt obligated to because he couldn't face the disapproval of his father. He may not have said the words, but she recognized the signs. And she couldn't ignore them.

God, Cash needs help. And I'm going to need Yours.

Because even if she had to endure the rest of the weekend with a good-looking, smooth-talking Texan, she was going to show Cash what it was like to truly live.

Chapter Four

Taryn's first stop Friday morning was the bank. She'd prayed and prayed, asking God to guide her on this decision and she was just as determined this morning, if not more so than she was when she lay down last night.

No doubt about it, All Geared Up was the perfect business for her. After all, Mr. Ramsey had hired her because of her extensive knowledge of outdoor gear. True, she only worked part-time, but she was the one who placed the orders, while he spent most of his time behind the counter. The icing on the cake, though, was the two apartments above the Main Street business. She could live in one and rent out the other.

But to make things happen, she'd need a loan. And she didn't have a clue what that entailed.

Moving through the double glass doors of Aspen Bank, she stepped onto the plush green carpet and scanned the open lobby. A long counter with several spaces for tellers stood at the back, a table laden with withdrawal and deposit slips was off to one side and a large reception desk sat opposite that.

"Good morning, Taryn." Patsy Weeks smiled from behind the desk. "What brings you by today?"

"Is Cam available?" Taryn had already spotted loan officer and long-time family friend Cam McAllister in his office.

"I believe so, but let me check." Patsy picked up the telephone receiver and punched a couple buttons. "Cam? Taryn Purcell would like to see you."

From the other end of the room, she could hear his booming voice. "Send her in."

Cam met her at his office door with a ready smile and a handshake. His bald head gleamed under the fluorescent lights. "To what do I owe this pleasure?"

"Well—" Suddenly nervous, she took a deep breath. "I'd like to talk to you about a business loan."

"That's what I'm here for." Stepping aside, he motioned her into his office. "Have a seat."

She eased into the burgundy wing-back chair while he closed the door and settled into the squeaky leather swivel chair behind his desk.

He leaned back, resting his folded hands atop his ample belly. "So, what are we looking at?"

"I don't know if you've heard or not, but Buck Ramsey is selling All Geared Up. I'd like to buy it."

The older man's brow lifted. "No. I hadn't heard that."

"He just told me yesterday morning, so maybe it isn't common knowledge."

"Well, don't you worry. What's discussed in this office stays in this office."

Since she hadn't even talked to her parents yet, that was a relief. "I appreciate that."

"So, do you know how much Buck is asking?"

"I do." She gave him the six-figure number. Though she hadn't asked Mr. Ramsey outright, she'd seen a flyer he'd printed.

"Do you have any collateral?"

"My Jeep. It's paid for. And I have about seven thousand in savings."

"I see." His chair creaked as he leaned forward, resting his arms on the glass-topped desk. "And how about a business plan?"

Anxiety took hold of her once again. "What's that?"

"All loan programs require a sound business plan to be submitted with the loan application. The plan should include a complete set of projected financial statements, including profit and loss, cash flow and a balance sheet."

"Oh." Her stomach churned. She tried not to look as clueless as she felt. Surely she could find something on the internet that would tell her how to put together a successful business plan.

"Do you have any management or business experience, Taryn?"

"Well, I—" *Sell yourself, girl.* "I work with people every day, Cam. I lead groups on climbing ventures, conduct workshops, and I've been at All Geared Up for over three years. I know that business inside and out."

He steepled his fingers, tapped them together, but didn't say a word.

This wasn't looking good.

Finally, he whirled his chair around to the credenza along the wall, opened the drawer and pulled out a large white envelope. Turning, he slid it across the desk. "The loan application is here, along with a checklist of everything we'll need from you before we can process things."

Her fingers shook as she reached for it. "Looks like this might take a while."

"It can be a bit confusing. But if you have any questions, feel free to give me a call."

"I will." Hugging the envelope to her chest, she stood. "Thank you for seeing me, Cam. I appreciate it."

"Not a problem, Taryn." He stood and rounded the desk.

"It's always good to see you." He opened the door, allowing the cooler air from the lobby to filter into the small space. "Tell your folks I said hi."

"I'll do that."

Getting into her Jeep, she breathed a sigh of relief. Step one, complete. She carefully laid the envelope on the passenger seat. With only a million more steps to go. How was she ever going to do this? She didn't know the first thing about a business plan.

Maybe she could ask Blakely. She had her own business. Of course, she'd inherited it from her grandfather. No business plan involved there.

The image of a handsome Texan popped into her head. Not the first time she'd thought of Cash today. Matter of fact, he'd littered her dreams all night. If anyone knew about business, it was Cash. He'd know exactly what to do.

Since Gramps barely knew what Wi-Fi was, let alone had it in his house, Cash made himself at home at a table in the backroom of a deli he found on Main Street. He needed to accomplish some work or he'd be completely behind when he got back to the office on Monday.

His first order of business had been that delayed shipment to Wiseman's. Turned out a big snowstorm in the northeastern part of the country had shut down roads, temporarily halting aluminum shipments, which, in turn, had slowed production.

After talking things over with his father, Cash phoned the distributor, explained the situation and offered a partial shipment. Wiseman's was happy, his father was happy, and that meant Cash was happy. Rubbing the back of his neck, he eyed the snow-covered peaks beyond the windows. Well, he was at least satisfied.

He took a sip of his coffee and perused Coble Trailers' latest sales figures. Better than he expected. With their new manufacturing facility, they were the largest supplier in the region. Before long, they'd be ready to go national.

"What do you think you're doing?"

Despite hitting a somewhat sour note during their walk last night, he couldn't help smiling when he saw Taryn staring down at him. Although, she didn't look nearly as happy to see him.

"Just getting a little work done."

"Did you accomplish anything?" Fists dug into her hips, she looked madder'n an old wet hen.

"A little. Yes."

"Good." She turned the laptop to face her, made a couple of clicks and closed the lid.

"What are you doing?"

She tucked the laptop under her arm. "Teaching you how to have fun."

With determined steps, she crossed the worn wooden floor, past the glass case filled with pastries and out the door. He shoved aside his mounting irritation and followed her outside.

She opened the door of a silver Jeep. "Hop in."

"Do I have a choice?"

"Not if you want to see your laptop again." She smiled at him.

Like he couldn't get it back if he wanted to. Strange thing was, he wasn't sure he really wanted to.

The midmorning sun emerged from a cloud, chasing the chill away as he climbed into the passenger seat. "What now?"

"Hang on and enjoy the ride." She pulled out onto Main Street and made a quick U-turn.

"How did you know where to find me?" He eyed the hot springs pool as they headed north.

"Your grandfather. Which reminds me, how dare you

leave him to go work? You only have a couple of days in town. Couldn't you at least devote your time to him?"

"Then why are you taking me in the opposite direction?"

"*I* have your grandfather's blessing. But he wants pictures."

"Pictures?" He jerked a look at her now. "Just where exactly are you taking me?"

Past Rotary Park, she turned off toward Lake Lenore and the Bachelor Syracuse, an old mine that now did tours, taking people inside the mountain and explaining what it was like to be a miner. "That's for me to know and you to find out."

The need to reprimand her taunting evaporated. On the contrary, he found her playfulness endearing.

He remained quiet while she maneuvered the narrow, tree-lined road, admiring the red sandstone formations in the distance. A fair amount of snow clung to the mountaintops and crevices. Nothing to write home about. Then he spotted the slab of ice that cascaded down the face of one of them.

He swallowed hard as they drew closer. His palms grew sweaty. "What are we doing?"

"It's a surprise."

"I'm not joking, Taryn." He couldn't hide the nervousness in his voice.

"Don't you trust me?" She brought the vehicle to a stop and looked at him.

Okay, maybe she didn't expect him to climb. Maybe she just wanted to show him what it was all about.

His gaze traveled up the frozen runoff. "Looks like that's my only option."

She exited the Jeep and he met her at the back of the vehicle. "I assume you're wearing comfortable clothes?"

He eyed his jeans and flannel shirt beneath his jacket. "Yes."

"Good." She opened the back gate and handed him a pair of pants and a fleece hoodie. "Amanda let me raid Randy's climbing gear. Since you two are about the same size, they should fit."

"Climbing gear?"

Lifting a brow, she sent him a look that told him questions were off-limits.

He returned to the front seat, dropped his cowboy boots in the snow and tugged on the insulated pants.

"You'll want these." She shoved a pair of heavy-duty hiking boots at him. "Let me know if they don't fit. I brought three different sizes."

Did she really expect him to climb?

He donned the first pair of boots without trouble, as well as the jacket, then tugged on the gloves and knit hat she also provided.

"Mr. Coble, you look mahvelous." Her smile of approval lifted his spirits. Still…

She held out a belt of some sort. "Now, shimmy into this harness—"

"Taryn, come on. You don't really expect me to ice climb, do you?"

Her smile only widened. "Yeah, I do."

"But, I—"

"Have a bad knee, I know. But that was a long time ago. And, according to my doctor friend, the only thing that limits you—" she strolled closer, determination sparkling in those icy eyes "—is you."

A physical blow couldn't have packed a bigger punch. Taryn was right and he knew it. His knee had made it easier to stay away from Ouray. Away from the mountains that begged to be climbed, away from the adventures waiting to be uncovered, away from the ice climbing he was once eager to try. All the things he longed to do on a regular basis but couldn't because he was stuck in Dallas.

She didn't back away. And the way she looked up at him…it made him feel as if he could do anything.

"What do you say?" She nodded her purple-beanie-covered head in the direction of the ice. "Shall we give it a try?"

In no time, he was harnessed, cramponed, helmeted and following an equally attired Taryn through the snow, up a narrow creek bed toward the icefall. Truth be told, in that moment, he probably would have followed her just about anywhere. Her gentle coaxing was hard to resist.

The occasional silvery-white cloud drifted overhead, obscuring the sun.

"Couldn't we have just gone to the ice park?"

"Nope." She pressed on.

"Why not?"

"I was afraid you'd try to escape."

By the time they reached the base of the slab, he was sweating. He eyed the stiff expanse of white towering over them. It wasn't nearly as smooth as he expected. More rippled, even lumpy in some spots.

Taryn dropped her backpack and the coil of rope she'd looped across her torso. "I'm going to have you wait here while I put in a few anchors. But first I want to show you a little technique so you can practice while I'm gone."

"Yeah, I wouldn't want to be bored."

Her grin only added to his anxiety. "Don't worry. You won't be."

She explained proper tool placement. How a single sure swing was better than chopping at the ice. "If you swing your tool too hard, your arms will tire quickly. We're not chopping down a tree."

"As for crampon technique…" She directed her attention to the spikes that'd been clamped onto the bottoms of their boots. "You not only want to engage the front teeth, but the second row as well. To do this, you have to drop your heels." She demonstrated. "It's tough on the calves, but I think you can handle it."

He did his best to duplicate the maneuver.

"Good. Just be sure to keep those heels low. Now, let's see you swing your tool."

"Align the shoulder, wrist and tool," he repeated then swung.

"Excellent." She rubbed a gloved finger over an indentation in the ice. "Look for depressions in the ice. They're stronger than bulges."

"Got it." At least he hoped so.

"Do you have any questions?"

"When can I get started?"

That earned him her brightest smile yet.

She stepped up to the ice. "Let me set these anchors and we'll get you going."

Tilting his head back, he watched her pick her way up the wall of ice. She definitely knew what she was doing. And in a matter of minutes, she was beside him once again, a rope running from her belay device up the steep slope and back to the ground.

She attached the other end of the rope to the device on his harness. "Are you ready?"

"I was born ready." He stepped up to the ice, not nearly as confident as he wanted Taryn to believe. Took a deep breath.

"Now, when you're going to start climbing, you say 'belay on.'"

"Belay on." He lifted his foot to jam his crampon into the ice—

"On belay."

"What?" He glanced over his shoulder.

"Means you're good to go."

"Oh." Apprehension knotted in his gut as he eyed the slippery slope once again. "You're sure this will hold me?"

"Yep."

"If you say so." He reached both tools over his head. Looked for indentations in the ice. Swung. Perfect. He dug his crampons into the ice and moved a couple steps before moving the first tool. Right hand. Right foot. Left hand. Left foot. He was doing it. He was actually ice climbing.

"Keep those heels down," Taryn hollered up at him.

He complied, his calves burning.

Right. Left. Right.

Pausing, he glanced down. He'd gone farther than he thought. He was a good thirty feet up. The sun broke through the clouds then, making it difficult to judge where to land his next swing. Too bad he didn't have his sunglasses. Then again, when he left the house, he'd had no intention of ice climbing.

He let 'er rip, little pieces of ice pelting his face.

Right foot.

Missed.

He tugged harder on the tool, but it wasn't secure.

Panic coursed through him as it slipped from the ice. His body tensed. He was going to fall.

Next thing he knew, he was swinging gently through the air, thanks to the belay.

"Everything okay up there?"

He struggled to catch his breath. "I think my life just flashed before my eyes."

"Was it worth watching?"

He couldn't help laughing. "Parts of it. Maybe."

Looking up, Taryn snapped a picture. "You might want to fix that."

Easy for her to say. She lived for the next climb. He lived for…

What did he live for?

He swung his tool. Landed it perfectly. He'd examine his pathetic life later. Right now, he needed to conquer this ice.

For the better part of two hours, he and Taryn took turns going up and down the ice.

"That's the most incredible, fulfilling thing I've done in a long time." Despite the cold, he was ready to shed his outer jacket. His body surged with energy and something he'd never felt before. "What did you call it?"

"Call what?"

"The feeling you get from climbing."

"Empowered."

"That's it." For the first time in more than a decade, Cash felt free. And he owed it all to the spunky girl next door. Without her, he'd still be staring at his laptop at the deli. But she'd drawn him into her world, given him a taste of what he'd been missing. And that was something he'd never forget.

Taryn loved this part of her job. The look on Cash's face was priceless. And she couldn't be more pleased with the way he'd put himself out there. His smile was unlike any she'd seen since he arrived. Genuine. He was truly enjoying himself.

She dropped her helmet.

"Does this mean we're done?" He watched her coil the rope.

"I'm afraid so." She sent him an apologetic look, just as sad as he was to see their time on the ice come to an end. "My best friend is getting married tomorrow and I'm the maid of honor, so I need to go help her."

"Seriously?" He pulled off his helmet, tucking it under his arm.

She nodded, stuffing their gear into her pack.

"Wow, thanks for bringing me out here then." He

grabbed the pack she'd loaned him. "I'm surprised you had any time at all."

"It's not a big wedding. And besides that, you need to get back to your grandfather."

"That reminds me, you did get some pictures of me, right?"

She couldn't help laughing. "Lots. I'll give you the memory card to upload to your computer. That way you can show your grandfather right away."

"Awesome."

"You got everything?" She eyed him as he slung his pack over his shoulder.

"I believe so." He stepped closer. "Why don't you let me take this." He lifted the rope from her and draped it across his torso. "Now we're ready."

The sun shone down on them as they headed to her Jeep.

"So tell me about the ice park," he said as they hiked. "Do a lot of locals go there?"

"Quite a few. It's kind of a social event."

"What do you mean?"

"You know, like a hangout. You want to catch up with people around town, that's the place to do it."

"Hmph. Interesting. Adds a whole new meaning to the term *watercooler*."

She chuckled. "That it does."

"Gramps mentioned an ice festival." Cash sounded as if he was getting a little winded, so she slowed her pace.

"Yep. The biggest one in North America."

"No kidding?"

"People come from all over the world to climb, test out the latest equipment and compete."

"Compete?"

"Oh, yeah. It's like the Olympics. There are a bunch of different events, and scores are announced in seven different languages." She adjusted her pack. "You should come to one."

"Maybe I will."

She shoved her hand in her pocket. Something crinkled beneath her gloved fingers. "Oh, I almost forgot." Pulling out the piece of paper, she held it out to him. "This is for you."

He glanced at her hand, then her face. "What is it?"

"The password to my parents' Wi-Fi." She handed it to him. "You should have a decent signal at your grandfather's, so you can now work from home."

"Taryn, you're lifesaver." He shoved the paper into the pocket of his jeans. "You have no idea how much this will help me."

"More importantly, you won't have to leave your grandfather."

"Precisely."

She sent him a sideways glance, anxiety suddenly getting the best of her. Should she even ask him for business advice? Well, nothing ventured, nothing gained. "I, um, don't suppose you know anything about business plans, do you?"

"Sure do. Had to assemble one before we built our new facility. Why?"

"I know someone who's looking at buying one of the businesses in town, and the bank says she has to put together a business plan before they'll consider her application."

"And does this someone have a name?" The look he gave her told her he already knew.

She took a deep breath. "All right, it's me. And, aside from the loan officer at the bank, you're the only one who knows, so please don't say anything to anyone. Not even your grandfather."

"I won't say a word." He tromped through the snow beside her, his quick breaths sending white puffs into the air. "So what kind of business are we talking about?"

"It's called All Geared Up and they sell almost any kind of gear the outdoor enthusiast might need." Relaxing, she eyed the man beside her. "I've worked there for the last three years."

His brow lifted. "So, no climbing, just the gear?"

"What do you mean?"

"Sorry, I just have a hard time imagining you stuck indoors, behind some sales counter."

"Hey, it might mean I can't do tours anymore, but nothing will ever stop me from climbing." She plodded alongside him. "Oh, and there are also two apartments upstairs. That means I can finally move out of Mom and Dad's, and I'll have income from the second space."

"That's part of your business plan right there." He dodged around a boulder.

"Really?"

"Yep."

"But what about all the financial stuff?"

"That needs to be in there, too. I'd be happy to help you, if you like."

"That'd be great, but—" She stopped.

He did too. "But what?"

"You're leaving Sunday. I'm tied up the rest of today and tomorrow."

"Hey, you know, they have these newfangled things called telephones. And email."

"Very funny." She reached out and gave him a shove, accidentally toppling him into a snowbank. "Oh!" She tried to stop herself from laughing. "Guess I don't know my own strength."

"All right, Purcell. You had your little chuckle. Now get over here and help me up." He held out his hand.

She closed the space between them and took hold. "Come on, cowboy." She tugged.

So did he. Next thing she knew, she was on the ground beside him.

"Oh, I can't believe I fell for that." Growing up with two older brothers, she should have known better.

"Me neither." Laughing, he tossed a handful of snow her way.

"Aw, man. Right down the neck." She squirmed as it began to melt against her skin. "Coble, you're a dead man."

As he hustled to stand, she fisted the back of his jacket, quickly depositing an icy chunk. "Let's see how you like it." She scrambled to her feet before he could retaliate.

"Ooo-wee, that feels good." He stood, trying to keep a smile.

"Yeah, I like that cute little dance you're doing." She thought she might bust a gut, watching him hop around, trying to untuck his shirt, all with that length of rope still around him. "Is that the Texas two-step?"

He sighed as the ice dropped to the ground. "All right, Purcell." He moved closer, but she took a step back. "I know when to admit defeat." He took another step and they were practically toe-to-toe. "You're a feisty one, you know that?"

"So I've been told." She dared to meet his appreciative look.

"Thank you for teaching this old dog some new tricks." He leaned closer until the fog of their breaths mingled.

She could smell the woodsy scent of his cologne. "Old dog?"

He grinned. "You know what I mean." He was so close. His gaze searched hers.

But she stepped away from him. "You're welcome, then." She nodded in the direction of her Jeep. "We'd better get going."

Chapter Five

By Saturday morning, Taryn had no doubt that the image of Cash's smile after scaling that ice would be forever seared into her memory. And that was not a good thing.

Yeah, she wanted to help the guy. Show him what he'd been missing in his life. But she hadn't counted on the feelings he stirred in her. Feelings she didn't want, because the last time she allowed herself to feel this way, her whole world shattered.

"You're unusually quiet this morning." Blakely shifted slightly in her spa chair, her strawberry-blond ponytail trailing over one shoulder. "What gives?"

Warm water bubbled around Taryn's feet as she sank deeper into her own spa chair, a pleasure she and Blakely rarely had the opportunity to revel in. Blakely owned Ouray's finest Jeep-tour company. As head grease monkey and guide extraordinaire, she, like Taryn, was a no-frills kind of girl. But that didn't mean they weren't in touch with their feminine side. So her friend's wedding day was the perfect opportunity to pull out all the stops. Manicure, pedicure, makeup and hair.

"Blakes, you're getting married. As your maid of honor, I have a right to be reflective."

"Not buying it." Blakely cocked her head. "Try again. Preferably, with the truth."

The two of them had always been brutally honest with each other. And Blakely was the only one who knew about Taryn's baby. She was the most trusted friend Taryn had ever had.

The people working in the salon were another matter, though.

But since they'd made themselves scarce for the moment… "Another long, tall Texan is tugging on my heartstrings."

Her friend's blue eyes lit up like an LED headlamp. "Are you kidding me? Who?"

"Easy, Blakes. It's nothing serious. Just a little…disconcerting."

"Okay, fine." Blakely whispered. "But will you at least tell me who you're talking about?"

She scanned the area, making sure no one was close enough to hear, then leaned toward her friend. "Mr. Jenkins's grandson, Cash."

"What happened?"

"You know how you're a sucker for that lost-puppy-dog look?"

"Yeah."

"Well, once I got past the fact that he looked and sounded so much like Brian…" She picked at her nonexistent fingernails, wondering what kind of magic Miranda could possibly work to make them look pretty. "It's like the guy has no life. Or a life not of his choosing."

"I'm not following you."

"He loves Ouray. Used to spend every summer here with his grandparents. But, until Thursday, he hasn't been back in ten years."

Blakely leaned closer. "Why?"

"He didn't say, but I have my suspicions. See, he took

over running his father's company when he got cancer. Even though he'd planned to move to Ouray. His father's okay now, but Cash is still there, doing everything he can to make his father proud."

"I see. So his hopes and dreams got sidetracked by the need to win his father's approval?"

"And it doesn't take a genius to see that it's robbed him of his joy." She scanned the tranquil and blessedly empty space once again. "Cash used to be a fun-loving and adventurous guy. Now he's always thinking about work. I'm not sure he even knows how to relax."

"And you're going to fix that."

Taryn tried not to smile but failed. "Well, I tried. I took him climbing yesterday."

"How did that go?"

"He loved it. And it was nice to see a glimpse of the old Cash."

"But…?"

"But nothing."

Blakely lifted a brow, soothing music filling the space between them.

"We're friends, Blakes."

"That could change."

"Not likely. He lives in Dallas. I live in Ouray. Long-distance relationships never work out."

Blakely crossed her arms over her chest. "Sometimes they do."

"Only if one party is willing to join the other. He's not going anywhere. And there's no way I'm ever setting foot in Texas again."

A smile played at the corners of her friend's mouth. "Never say never, Taryn. That's just enough to make the good Lord show you who's boss."

"Okay, ladies. Have your tootsies thawed out?" Miranda, the salon's owner, emerged from the back room.

Blakely straightened, adjusting the pillow in her lap. "Mine have."

"I'm good," said Taryn.

"Sally." Miranda motioned for her assistant before addressing Blakely and Taryn. "Thought we'd get your toes done first so they'll be good and dry by the time you're ready to put your boots back on. It's really coming down out there."

Taryn and Blakely looked out the front window, stunned to discover the snow had really picked up.

"Wow. It was barely flurrying when we got here." Taryn couldn't help thinking about Cash. Looked like he got his wish for snow. Hopefully, he was enjoying it and not staring at his computer. Maybe she should call Mr. Jenkins and ask him. But what would Cash think about her checking up on him?

The guy is leaving tomorrow.

May as well go for the gusto.

She tugged her cell phone from the back pocket of her jeans and dialed her neighbor. Luckily, Miranda, Sally and Blakely were engrossed in nail color selections and not paying attention to her.

"Mr. Jenkins." She kept her voice as low as possible. "Is Cash around?"

"Sure is. Taryn wants to talk to you." His voice faded as he handed off the phone.

"Hello."

"Are you looking out the window?"

"I'll do you one better. I just came in the house to get warm. I've been outside enjoying every flake."

"No kidding?" Perhaps she'd made some progress, after all.

"Wish you were here. We could build a snowman."

"Snowman? There can't be more than two inches on the ground."

Blakely held a bottle of nail polish in front of her and pointed to her toes. It was the same wine color as her dress. She smiled and shot her friend a thumbs-up.

"In Texas we make snowmen with a lot less snow than that."

"They must be awful small."

"Hey, it's about the experience."

She turned away from the other women. "Who are you and what have you done with Cash?"

"Very funny."

"Afraid you're on your own for this one, cowboy. I'm enjoying a day of pampering at the spa."

"Will I see you later?"

Suddenly a swarm of butterflies came to life in her stomach. "Are you coming to the wedding with your grandfather?"

"I am."

That meant he'd see her all dressed up. In high heels and a dress. Makeup, nails, hair…

The butterflies multiplied.

Tomorrow couldn't come soon enough.

After only two days in Ouray, Cash was happier than he'd been in ages. Now, as he and Gramps stepped through the doors of Restoration Fellowship, he couldn't ignore his eagerness to see Taryn. The woman fascinated him.

Beyond the small foyer, candlelight flickered throughout the small sanctuary while music drifted from an acoustic guitar. White tulips adorned both sides of the altar, continuing in front of the piano and organ. Simple decorations, but stunning nonetheless.

The snow had stopped over an hour ago, but Cash still insisted they drive the few blocks to the church. Virtually everything in Ouray was within walking distance, but dressed in nice clothes, he wasn't about to invite disaster.

He and Gramps were seated on the groom's side, though Gramps was quick to let him know he was friends with both the bride and the groom. Apparently everyone in town was eager to celebrate the union of these two people. The pews were filling faster than a creek in a gully washer.

According to Taryn, the bride and groom fell in love one long-ago summer. Then he'd gone on to marry someone else. Ten years later, he came back, widowed, and surprised not only to find Blakely, but a son he never knew existed. God had brought the three of them back together and they were finally going to be a family.

A wistfulness had filled Taryn's eyes when she told the story. A look that seemed to go beyond being happy for her friend.

Cash noticed an older woman being escorted to the front pew on the bride's side.

Gramps leaned closer. "That's Blakely's grandmother, Rose Daniels," he whispered. "Owns the Alps Motel."

The minister, groom and a young boy Cash guessed was the couple's son appeared at the front. A moment later, the notes of a classical tune floated through the air.

Rustling behind him captured his attention. He turned and, at the back of the church, saw Taryn waiting. She wore a strapless dress the color of red wine that accented her small waist. On cue, she started down the aisle in high-heeled silver sandals with a grace that belied the tomboy image he'd seen yesterday. Talk about the total package. This girl was it.

He swallowed hard as she walked past him. Her short golden-brown hair was tucked behind one ear, while the other side framed her beautiful face.

When Taryn reached the altar, the wedding march started, the doors at the back of the room swung open and the congregation stood.

Blakely was a cute strawberry-blonde with a smile as big as Texas. Seemed she didn't have eyes for anyone but her intended as she strode down the aisle solo.

Shifting his attention to the groom, Cash saw the same love and adoration on his face as he watched his bride move toward him.

Cash thought back on his relationship with Yvette. Had he ever inspired that kind of look from her?

No. Nor had she from him. Yet his father had been convinced Yvette would make the perfect wife. So, like the dutiful son, Cash had given it his best shot. In the end, Yvette had realized Cash was not the man for her.

Now he was glad she'd turned down his proposal. He never should have proposed in the first place. He shifted in his seat. Just one more failed attempt to live up to his father's expectations.

He wondered if he'd ever find that kind of love. He hoped so, but life held no guarantees. Still, if he found the right woman, maybe things would be different, maybe he would be different.

"Dearly beloved, we are here today to celebrate the union of Trent and Blakely…" The pastor prayed and the guests were seated.

Cash didn't pay much attention to the ceremony. He was too busy staring at Taryn. If he had seen her looking like this the first time he met her, he would have thought she was just another North Dallas beauty queen. But this was definitely not the down-to-earth Taryn he'd gotten to know over the last couple days.

Suddenly, she set down her bouquet and picked up a microphone. Music played through the speakers and Taryn began to sing.

Closing his eyes, he listened to her voice. Delicate, yet strong. Moving. Not unlike the woman behind it. The one who had urged him to step out of his comfort zone. Showing him what was missing from his life.

Which was something he had never expected.

In the main room of the community center, the bride and groom took the floor for their first dance as husband and wife. Blakely looked stunning in her wedding dress, a simple lace, strapless gown with just a hint of a train. Trent clearly adored Blakely. And their son, Austin, was ecstatic to have his father.

Taryn found herself swaying to the romantic country tune that played.

God, will anyone ever love me like that? Until recently, she'd been content to be alone. But seeing Blakely so happy unearthed those schoolgirl notions of love and happily ever after. Dreams she thought she'd buried a long time ago.

Scanning the tables of guests, she saw Mr. Jenkins talking with Blakely's grandmother. But Cash was nowhere to be seen. He'd probably decided to cut out after the wedding. After all, with his grandfather occupied, he could work all he wanted without feeling guilty.

Still, a part of her wished he was here. He'd be leaving in the morning. She'd at least like the chance to say goodbye.

"You look like you could use some punch." A cup appeared in front of her, the hand holding it attached to Cash.

Her heart pounded an alarm, but one look at Cash and the warning bells faded. "I thought maybe you'd gone back to your grandfather's." She accepted the drink. Took a sip.

"And miss an opportunity to dance with you? My mama didn't raise no dummy."

She couldn't help laughing and was amazed that she'd actually come to appreciate his Texas drawl. It suited him. It wasn't forced. Just natural and uniquely Cash.

"Aren't they a lovely couple?" Taryn's mother sashayed

up to Cash, that matchmaking gleam in her eye. Giving Taryn more than enough reason to be nervous.

"They are indeed, Bonnie."

"You know…" Her mother leaned closer. "When Taryn was a little girl, she told me she was going to marry you someday."

"Mother!" Taryn always knew her mother possessed the capability to embarrass her. But this was beyond anything she could have imagined.

Cash's mischievous grin tempered her anger. "Oh, did she now?"

Good thing the lights were dim, because her cheeks had to be bright red. "I was ten years old. I was into Barbie and princesses."

People clapped as the song ended, and Trent and Blakely approached as a more up-tempo tune coaxed others onto the dance floor.

"And why didn't my maid of honor join us?" asked Blakely.

"I don't think the best man is interested in dancing," she said.

Trent laughed. "Give him a few more years."

"That Austin will be a heartbreaker someday," said her mother. "Trent, have you met Cash?"

His attention shifted to the man beside her. "I have not. Cash, is it?"

Cash held out his hand. "Yes. Cash Coble. Nice to meet you."

"He's Art Jenkins's grandson," her mother was quick to inject.

"Hi, Cash. I'm Blakely."

"You own the Jeep-tour place, right?"

"*We* do." She motioned to her husband. "You'll have to come back next summer and let us take you for a ride."

"Sounds like fun."

"Mom. Dad." Austin hurried toward them, his black patent-leather shoes slapping against the wooden floor.

"Hey, short man," said Blakely.

"You missed your chance to dance with your date," added Trent.

Austin glanced at Taryn, his cheeks ruddy. "Sorry." He turned his attention back to his parents. "Zach and I were outside. It's snowing like crazy."

Everyone followed his gaze out the window. Sure enough, the snow had started up again, even heavier than before.

Trent tugged Blakely against him. "Good thing we decided to stay in town tonight."

The DJ played another slow song. "This one is ladies' choice."

Her mom's gaze bounced between Cash and Taryn. "Honey, if you're not going to ask him, I might have to."

And give her mother another chance to embarrass her? No way. Taryn held out a hand. "Care to dance?"

He escorted her onto the dance floor. Then he took her into his arms and she thought she might melt. He felt strong and solid.

She tried to relax but was afraid she might enjoy this dance just a little too much.

"Don't worry, I won't hold you to it." His breath was warm on her ear.

She dared a look at those deep green eyes. "What's that?"

"About marrying me."

Her face grew warm. "I have never been so embarrassed in my life."

He laughed.

"You think this is funny?"

"I think that cute glow you get when you're embarrassed is funny."

She rolled her eyes. "I should have left you to my mother."

His hold tightened. "No. I like this much better."

The music played on and, despite her best intentions, Taryn wished it would never end.

But she knew it would end. She pulled away from him. "I need to check in with the caterer."

Thanks to the rapidly falling snow, the crowd had dwindled earlier than expected. Trent and Blakely had gone to their suite at the Beaumont Hotel. Taryn's mom and dad went home shortly thereafter. The DJ was packing his gear while Taryn helped a couple of women from the church clean up. They'd insisted Rose go on home and leave them to finish.

Across the room, she noticed Cash clearing tables. She thought she'd seen Mr. Jenkins leave and assumed Cash had gone with him. But there he was, making her job a lot easier.

"You didn't have to stay," she said as he dumped a handful of cups and plates in the trash.

"I thought I'd escort you home." His eyes skimmed over her. "You're not exactly dressed for the weather."

"I have my Jeep and a coat."

"You realize you're wearing sandals?"

She observed her freshly painted toes. "Guess I'll just have to make a run for it."

With the reception area clean, Cash helped her with her coat and, despite her objections, held tight to her hand as he walked her to the car.

"I should have thought to warm it up for you," he said, sliding into the passenger side.

"That's okay. We're not going that far." Four blocks, to be exact.

When she pulled up to her house, the porch light was on. But the snow was six inches deep across the walk.

"Yep, those pretty little toes of yours are going to get mighty cold." Cash quickly assessed the situation…. "Or not. Stay right there."

He exited the vehicle and ran around to her side. Opened her door. "In the name of chivalry, there's only one thing to do."

"What's that?"

"I'm going to carry you."

"Carry me? Oh, no."

"Oh, yes." He held out his arms.

She lifted a brow. "You're not serious. Are you?"

"Dead serious."

She'd really like to argue with him, but it was too cold. She pulled the key from the ignition. "Suit yourself."

He scooped her into his arms and she pushed the door closed behind them.

"Go around back." Freezing-cold air swept over her bare legs. "If my mother sees us, I'll never hear the end of this."

He glanced at the house. "Looks pretty dark in there to me."

She recalled her mother waiting in the dark for her on more than one occasion during Taryn's high school years. "You obviously don't know my mother."

He stepped carefully through the ever-accumulating snow as more clung to their coats, hair and eyelashes. "How long is this snow supposed to last?"

"I don't know. I didn't think they were forecasting this much."

"Guess I'd better head out early tomorrow. Give myself plenty of time to get to Durango."

"You know, you could have flown into Montrose."

"I waited too late. They were sold out."

"Next time, you'll have to plan ahead."

Was it her imagination, or did he just frown? Perhaps

he was getting tired of carrying her. Luckily, they were at the back steps.

He lowered her onto the porch. "Here we go. Safe and sound."

"Thank you. But you really didn't have to carry me."

"You're welcome." He stared at her for what seemed like forever. "You're a very intriguing woman, Taryn Purcell."

"Who, me?"

"You're fun, adventurous…you don't back down from a challenge." He cocked his head. "But you're also gentle and sweet, not to mention drop-dead gorgeous."

She forgot to breathe as he cupped her cheek. Images of another Texan tinted her vision.

"Thank you again for reminding me what it's like to live." His gaze fell to her lips. He leaned toward her.

"No!" She pushed at his chest and took a giant step back. This wasn't happening again. "You Texans are all alike."

His eyes went wide. He probably wasn't used to being refused.

"You think your sweet talk and charm will have women falling at your feet. Then you kick them to the curb." She turned and reached for the door. "Goodbye, Cash."

Chapter Six

Darkness still prevailed when Cash quietly navigated his way down Gramps's stairs Sunday morning. Behind the glass fireplace doors, blue-and-orange flames danced and crackled, suffusing the living room with warmth.

Cash breathed in the subtle aroma of burning wood. No wonder he never used the gas fireplace in his apartment. Not only was it rarely cold enough, it just wasn't the same.

A light glowed from the kitchen, telling him his grandfather was awake.

Cash set his small rolling suitcase by the front door and headed toward the smell of fresh-brewed coffee. Maybe Gramps would have a travel mug he could take with him. He'd need all the caffeine he could get. Thoughts of Taryn had kept him awake much of the night. What had he been thinking, attempting to kiss her? He certainly hadn't intended to. But it felt so right.

Boy, was he wrong.

Gramps had said that Taryn was different when she returned to Ouray. And as her parting words replayed in Cash's mind countless times, he'd come to one conclusion. Whatever change had taken place in Taryn had to do with Texas.

"Morning, Gramps," he said, entering the kitchen.

His grandfather sat in his usual spot on the side of the table that afforded him a view of the old console television in the living room. Maybe Cash should consider getting him another TV for his birthday. A flat-screen he could have mounted on the wall in the kitchen. Or, perhaps, a bigger one for the living room.

His grandfather lowered his Bible, took off his reading glasses. "Mornin'."

Cash opened the cupboard and searched. Finding no lidded cup, he grabbed the largest mug there was, then reached for the coffeepot.

"Son, I don't suppose I could talk you into staying another day or so, could I?"

He faced his grandfather, knowing he couldn't possibly afford any more time away from the office. Not to mention risk seeing Taryn. "Why? Is something wrong?"

"Have you looked outside this morning?"

"Not yet." Mug in hand, he moved to the back door, flipped on the porch light and fingered the ruffled yellow curtain to one side.

The pine tree at the back of the yard bowed under the weight of no less than ten inches of snow.

"It must have snowed all night." And it was still coming down, though not nearly as hard.

"I believe it did."

Cash let the curtain fall back into place. "Good thing I got up earlier than planned. It's going to be slow going over those passes." He took a swig of coffee.

"About that." Gramps folded his arms on the table as Cash sat across from him. "I've already checked with the sheriff's department and the passes are still open. But they're apt to close them at any time."

"What do you mean? That's a main highway. How can they just close it down?"

"Happens all the time during the winter. When you're talking about four to five feet of snow up in the mountains, the possibility of an avalanche is too great to chance."

"Guess I'd better get going then. Give myself plenty of time." Because he had to get back to Dallas. And he couldn't do that if he couldn't get to Durango.

His grandfather shrugged, but Cash could see the old man's disappointment. "I understand. But you better take it mighty slow. Low gear. Don't get in a hurry."

"Yes, sir." He sent his grandfather a reassuring smile and held up his cup. "Mind if I take this with me?"

"'Course not." The old man eased to his feet and followed him to the door. "It's sure been a pleasure having you here again. Like old times."

Cash couldn't argue and was surprised by the emotion that thickened his throat.

He cleared it away. "Maybe I can make it back this summer."

"Fourth of July's always good."

He smiled at his grandfather, recalling the fire-hose water fights and the fireworks that reverberated through the canyon. "I'll see what I can do."

Thirty minutes after saying goodbye to Gramps, Cash understood the old man's concern. He'd never driven in weather like this. Low clouds enveloped a snow-packed Highway 550, and the higher he climbed, the harder the snow came down. With so many curves and sheer drop-offs, he had barely made it out of Ouray.

How did people drive in this stuff? Then again, it wasn't as if the road was filled with cars. He probably hadn't counted more than two or three.

Inching up Red Mountain Pass, Cash downshifted again. The windshield wipers beat out a steady rhythm while the defroster struggled to keep things melted and warm. He continued to watch the taillights of the SUV several car lengths in front of him. Taillights that suddenly brightened. Even he knew better—

Before he completed the thought, the other vehicle went into a spin.

Tightening his grip on the steering wheel, he instinctively hit the brakes. A move he immediately regretted. The wheels locked. He heard a beeping sound and a light flashed on the dashboard. The vehicle skidded.

He removed his foot and the rental quickly recovered.

Breathing a sigh of relief, he again focused on the out-of-control vehicle ahead.

"Oh, no. No. No!" Adrenaline coursed through his veins as the other vehicle slid across the northbound lane, becoming airborne before tumbling down the steep embankment.

His pulse raced as he struggled to bring his SUV to a stop. He checked the rearview mirror. No one behind him. He scanned the horizon. No one ahead either.

He fumbled for his cell from the console beside him. Dialed 911. "Come on…"

Silence was all he heard. He looked at the screen. No service.

"Lord, what do I do?"

The blue button at the base of the rearview mirror captured his attention. He could only pray it worked.

He pressed it, his anxiety ratcheting up a notch as he scanned the snowy ravine for the wayward vehicle. *Please, Lord, let them be alive.*

"How may I help you?" A voice came through the car's speakers.

"Hello. Yes." *Concentrate, Coble. They need details.* With a calm he didn't feel, he relayed his location and information about the accident as succinctly as possible.

Confident that assistance was on the way, he turned on his hazard lights, emerged from the vehicle and rushed to the spot where the car had gone over. The bitter cold stung his eyes and ears. Snow pelted his cheeks as he scanned the steep embankment. Dawn had begun to overtake the darkness, aiding his search.

He spotted debris and followed the path of fresh-packed snow deeper and deeper into the ravine. Hundreds of feet beneath him, the SUV lay on its side in what appeared to be a creek bed.

He cringed. This did not look good. But he couldn't wait around to find out.

Fisting the gloves from each of his jacket pockets, he tugged them on and started down the embankment.

Taryn reached for the cell phone on her nightstand and pressed a button to illuminate the screen: 6:55. Later than she expected.

Scout snored under the covers, pressed against the small of Taryn's back, where she'd been most of the night.

At least one of them had slept. Whether her eyes were closed or open, all Taryn could see was Cash. And the look on his face when she'd turned on him last night.

Ugh! What had she been thinking?

She'd been thinking about Brian, that's what. Suddenly she was eighteen again, and very foolish.

Rolling over, she adjusted the down comforter and tugged Scout against her chest.

The dog groaned.

Taryn responded with a sigh of her own. "Scout, your mommy is losing her mind."

Cash was not Brian. His attempted kiss was born of nothing more than gratitude. He was simply thanking her for the fun they'd had together.

Yet she'd made him out to be a bad guy. Ruining what had been an otherwise wonderful evening. It had been a long time since she'd felt so…wanted. Pretty. Vulnerable. Like maybe someone could love her.

Her dog stretched and licked Taryn's face.

She owed Cash another apology. But he was on his way back to Dallas.

And probably thinking she was a crazy woman.

Her pager beeped, interrupting her thoughts.

Tossing the comforter aside, she snagged the device as she sat up.

Vehicle off road near Red Mountain Pass. Meet at barn.

Familiar with the routine, she dressed quickly. Members of Ouray Mountain Rescue were available 24/7 for call-outs that ranged from high- and low-angle rescues, to swift water emergencies, and searches.

Pausing at the window, she opened the blinds. Even though the sun wouldn't top the peaks of the Amphitheater for another hour and a half, the thick clouds reflected off the fresh snow, illuminating everything. With this much snow in town, no telling how bad it was in the mountains.

She turned to grab her pack. Too bad this hadn't come a day or two earlier. Cash would have loved it.

Her heart dropped. *Cash.* He'd have driven over Red Mountain Pass.

She looked back to the window, to the house next door. The rented SUV was gone.

Oh, dear Lord, please let Cash be okay.

Taryn stared out the window of the rescue truck, watching the snow grow deeper and deeper. All the while, her heart pounded faster. She took a deep breath, tried to level out her pulse. She was a professional. What were the odds that Cash was involved in this accident anyway?

He's from Dallas. He doesn't know how to drive in this kind of weather.

Red-and-white lights flashed through the cloudy haze as they approached the scene.

"Looks like Silverton Fire beat us." Nolan Dickerson, the team captain, eased the truck to the side of the road.

Taryn exited and hurried across the snowy road to survey the wreckage. A white SUV lay at the bottom of the canyon. Not a blue SUV like the one Cash had driven.

While her anxiety eased, there were people who still needed their help.

She joined Nolan and the other dozen or so team members as they talked with one of the firefighters.

"There's a husband and wife and a couple kids. Not sure the extent of the injuries. A passerby saw the whole thing and stopped to help. Good thing, too. A white vehicle like that might not have been spotted for days."

Passerby?

"Yeah, especially now that they've closed the pass." Nolan scanned the surrounding peaks, each heavy with snow. "From the looks of things, no one will be coming through here for a few days."

"You said someone stopped to help?" She eyed the firefighter.

"Some fella on his way to Durango. I think he's still down there." He pointed to the wreckage, but it was too far away and with the snow still falling, she couldn't tell who was who.

Stepping away from the group, she rounded the fire truck and stopped.

How did she know?

Because Cash is a good guy.

His blue SUV sat covered with snow, red taillights flashing in warning.

She hurried back to the group as Nolan made assignments. "I'll go down."

Everyone looked at her.

"He said there are kids, right?" Cash wasn't the only one she had a soft spot for. "You know I can get down there faster than anyone."

"All right," said Nolan. "Matt, you go too."

They donned helmets, vests and harnesses and each grabbed a hefty length of rope. As soon as everything was secured, they began their descent.

Cash had never been so cold in his entire life. Snow had come up to his hips in places. He had no hat and his jacket definitely wasn't made for anything below freezing. Still, he couldn't leave this poor family until he knew they would be okay.

The father, who'd been driving the vehicle, was unconscious when Cash first made it to them, blood seeping from a small wound on the man's forehead. The woman in the passenger seat had teetered between dazed and completely freaked out, while the two kids had cried in the backseat. Thankfully, both had been strapped in their car seats.

Through sometimes chattering teeth, Cash had done his best to talk to them, keep them calm and assess the situation. What he couldn't do, though, was get to them. The windows, while cracked, were still intact and none of the doors would budge. It was going to take the Jaws of Life to get these folks out.

"Mountain Rescue's here." The EMT who had joined him not more than ten minutes ago nodded toward the road.

Mountain Rescue? "Would that be Ouray Mountain Rescue?"

"Only one I know of."

That meant Taryn would likely be with them. A wave of both apprehension and excitement ran through him.

"We won't know for sure until we get them out—" the

EMT stepped closer, keeping his voice low "—but these are some lucky folks. I wasn't sure what we'd find."

"Yeah, I know." Cash had prayed the entire way that no one would be seriously injured. Or worse. Once the father came to, though, Cash felt better about things.

"Here they come." The EMT nodded behind Cash.

The rattle of carabiners grew louder as the two helmeted people wearing red jackets pushed their way through the snow. One much shorter than the other. With extraordinary blue eyes.

His heart thundered. A part of him was ecstatic to see her, while the rest of him filled with dread.

Her gaze bore into him, yet instead of the playfulness he'd grown accustomed to seeing, she was strictly business. Nothing that indicated she was mad at him. Was she surprised to see him? Did she even care?

"We're going to need an extraction team," said the EMT. "These doors ain't budging."

"How are the kids?" Taryn looked from the EMT to Cash.

"Scared," said Cash.

"I can imagine." She moved to the vehicle. "Matt, radio topside. Tell them what we need."

"Their names are Bobby and Jenny," Cash told her.

She smiled back. "Thanks."

"You the one who stopped to help?" Taryn's counterpart stood in front of him.

"I think anybody would have done the same thing."

"Oh, you'd be surprised." The fellow held out a gloved hand. "Thanks, man."

Over the next several minutes, more people descended into the ravine, carrying basket gurneys and various other equipment.

Cash was given a harness and instructed which rope to use for his ascent. If he thought he was cold before, now he was downright frozen. His muscles were weak and his legs refused to cooperate at times. But with the help of those on the other end of his line, he made it and was greeted with a blanket and some hot coffee.

"That your SUV?" Another member of the rescue team pointed to his snow-covered rental.

"Yes, sir."

"Thing's probably stone cold by now. You look like you could use someplace warm."

"I think you're right." Cash couldn't stop shaking.

"I'm Nolan Dickerson." The man escorted him to the rescue truck.

"C-Cash Coble."

"You did a good thing today, Cash." Nolan opened the door and helped Cash inside the cab. "If it weren't for you, we might not have found those folks."

Nolan held up a metal thermos. "There's plenty more coffee in here, so help yourself." He started to close the door.

"I was on my way to Durango. I'm supposed to catch a flight back to Dallas."

"Afraid you won't make it, Cash. They've closed the pass."

"Closed? When will it be open?"

"Three days. Maybe more." Nolan's gaze skimmed the sky. "Depends on Mother Nature."

Sitting in the rescue truck, Cash let his head drop against the headrest. Three days? Dad was not going to be happy.

Cash stared out the window. He'd definitely gotten his wish for snow. Though it didn't look like he'd be enjoying any of it with Taryn.

Taryn watched the ambulance pull away, grateful that everyone involved in the crash had only minor injuries.

Had Cash not witnessed the accident and taken action, she had no doubt this would have ended as a recovery instead of a rescue. And she was a sucker for happy endings.

She was on her way back to the rescue truck when the door opened and Cash emerged.

A giant lump formed in her throat.

His face and ears were still red, though not as bright as they'd been before. But against that blond hair… He looked a little wobbly, too, reaching for the door to steady himself.

"You gonna be okay to drive there, Cash?" Nolan's brow knit with concern.

Concern she shared. Cash wasn't used to this kind of cold. Nor was he dressed for it. Yet he'd spent who knows how long down there, watching over total strangers. Anyone would have been spent.

"I'll drive him."

Nolan looked at her with a smirk.

"He's Art Jenkins's grandson. He's staying right next door to me."

"Ah." Nolan's gaze went to Cash. "Well, I'm sure your grandfather will be very proud of what you did today."

Silverton Fire pulled away from the scene at the same time Mountain Rescue headed the opposite direction. The snow was still coming down and Taryn found herself having to hold on to Cash as they made their way to his rental.

"The cold can really zap your strength."

"That's for sure." He smiled weakly. "I feel like a wet noodle."

"You were the one who wanted to see snow. Guess you got your wish." She held out her hand. "Keys?"

"Hmm? Oh." He dug into the pocket of his jeans and handed them over.

Emotions had run high today, as they did for any rescue. But they usually didn't involve someone who had the potential to steal her heart. Standing here now, looking at Cash, fear, anger, relief and something she wasn't even going to try to name blended into one overwhelming reaction.

"What were you thinking, attempting to drive to Durango?" She shoved him against the side of the SUV, emotions getting the best of her. "You know nothing about driving in weather like this." She whacked his arm. "You're lucky it wasn't you who went over that cliff." Tears welled in her eyes as she poked her finger into his chest.

Then, before she could stop herself, she thrust her arms around his waist and fell into his embrace. He smelled like coffee and hard work. And despite the cold, he was warm.

With a deep breath, she pulled herself together and backed away.

His green eyes searched hers. "What was that for?"

"For being a hero."

Chapter Seven

"I tried, Dad, but they're saying the pass will be closed for two to three days." Cash scrubbed a hand over his face and stared out the kitchen window at a sea of white. He couldn't believe all that had transpired this morning. And while Warren Coble may be used to getting his way, even he couldn't undo the forces of nature.

"I hate winter. Slows down progress." His father's exaggerated sigh crackled through the line.

"Things'll be fine." Cash moved toward the coffeepot for another cup. "I've got my phone and laptop, so I can work from here."

"What about the factory?"

Cash rarely set foot in the factory. Manufacturing was Dad's territory. "You'll be fine."

Another sigh. "I'm getting too old for this." He could imagine his dad scratching a hand through his neatly combed salt-and-pepper hair.

"No, you're not." Leaning against the counter, he cradled the warm mug in one hand. "So we have to change things up a bit. Change can be good, you know."

"Since when?"

The man was impossible.

"I never should have let your mother talk me into letting you go."

If there was one opponent his father couldn't stand against, it was Cash's mother. Elise Coble knew her husband inside and out. The woman could talk him into making a bonfire in hundred-degree temperatures.

"Well, we can't change things now, so we'll just have to go with the flow. I'll get back there just as soon as I can."

"I think I'll have Millie check flights out of Montrose first thing tomorrow. See if we can get you home a little sooner."

Cash shook his head. Dad's administrative assistant wielded almost as much power over Dad as Cash's mother. "All right, Dad. Talk to you later."

He tucked the phone into his pocket and took another sip of coffee, relieved to have that out of the way. Now maybe he could think about doing some work. With access to the Purcells' Wi-Fi, he could set up a makeshift office at the house.

Strolling into what had once been the dining portion of the living/dining room combo, he eyed the drop-leaf table tucked against the wall. Formal dinners had become a thing of the past after his grandmother passed away.

A scraping noise drew his attention to the window just beyond the table. He shoved the sheer panel aside to investigate. The snow had stopped, but the weight had a large branch bowing across the driveway.

"It's that blasted pine limb rubbing against the house." Gramps looked away from the basketball game on TV. "Happens every time we get a lot of snow. I keep forgetting to trim it."

"I'll take care of it, Gramps." He continued into the living room. "It'll give me something to do tomorrow."

"I guess your father's not too pleased with the situation."

"Of course not." Cash steadied his mug as he eased into his grandmother's old rocker recliner on the other side of the fireplace. "I mean, I'm not thrilled about it, either, but what am I supposed to do?" He started to take a sip then realized what he'd said. "No offense, Gramps."

"None taken. But let me ask you this—" Gramps muted the television "—why is it so important to get back? I mean, what's a couple more days?" His green eyes held Cash's as he sipped his own drink.

"Because…it's work. It's what I do. People rely on me to be there."

"You ever hear the expression all work and no—"

"Play…yeah, I've heard it." He set his cup on the small side table. "More times than I care to."

"Ever think there might be something to it?" His grandfather's scrutiny was a little unnerving. "You know, God often speaks to us in repetition. Especially when we have a hard time hearing."

"What are you saying, Gramps?"

"I'm saying I don't believe in coincidence. I think the good Lord's keeping you here for a reason." The old man dropped his footrest.

"What reason?"

"Maybe you work too hard." His grandfather leaned forward, resting his forearms on his thighs. "When was the last time you went to church?"

"Christmas."

"And before that?"

Cash struggled to remember. "Easter?"

Wow. When did that happen? He knew he'd quit going every Sunday, needing to work instead. But he didn't think his visits had grown that few and far between. "I still tithe."

"Tithing isn't just about money, Cash." His grandfather leaned back again, hands folded across his belly. "It's about our time, too. Giving back to God. Since you're not giving, maybe He decided you needed a little nudge."

"I've been here since Thursday."

"True. And I've enjoyed every minute of it. But—" he held up a crooked finger "—and I want you to answer this honestly, not what you think I want to hear—where has your focus been?"

Man, did he feel like a jerk. "On work."

Gramps winked. "Maybe not a hundred percent." He poked a thumb toward the window. "I believe that little filly next door managed to steal some of your focus."

Thoughts of ice climbing and their time at the wedding reception had Cash unable to hide his grin. "She's something special, all right." Perplexing, too. After reading him the riot act both last night and on the mountain…she hugged him. Then remained quiet the entire ride home. And once they made it to the house, she seemed eager to disappear next door.

Gramps grew serious again. "Tell me, Cash, how is your relationship with the Lord?"

He retrieved his mug and sipped the now-lukewarm brew while he gave some thought to the question. He would like to think he was a good Christian, but when was the last time he'd really talked to God or sought His guidance?

Today, of course, when the situation was completely out of his hands. But aside from that…?

He set his cup down. "Truthfully…it's pretty much comprised of arrow prayers." Those shot up when things got tough.

Gramps nodded, his lips pressed into a thin line. "The way I see it, you can fight this time God has given you, or you can use it to get reacquainted with Him. I'll let you work, but keep the Lord at the forefront of all you do, Cash. You might be surprised what He has to say."

Cash reclined his chair and closed his eyes, ashamed

that he'd allowed other things to crowd God out of his life. *Forgive me, Lord.*

When he opened his eyes, he realized he'd fallen asleep. Evidently he was more tired than he thought.

"Have a nice nap?"

Cash lowered the footrest, stood. "Sure did." He stretched. "Felt pretty good, too."

"Well, after what you went through this morning, I reckon you deserved it." Gramps turned up the volume on the second basketball game of the day.

"How long was I out?"

"'Bout an hour, hour and a half."

"Really?" There were some nights he didn't get much more than that. And he couldn't remember the last time he'd had a nap. Whatever the case, work was not happening today.

Stopping at the window, he stared at the house next door. Was Taryn still upset with him?

He roughed a hand across his face. He owed her an apology.

"Looks like the kids are all headed over to Vinegar Hill." Gramps peered out the front window.

Two boys trudged past, carrying sleds. Though the snow had long since stopped, the sun had yet to shine. But that wasn't about to stop those boys. And who could blame them? Even Cash wanted to get out and play in it.

"That's over between Fifth and Sixth Avenues, right?"

"Sure is." His grandfather faced him now, a smile creasing his face. "You thinking 'bout doing some sledding?"

It did sound rather enticing. "Think I could get a certain someone to join me?" Grinning, he donned a coat from Gramps's closet. Not the height of fashion and the sleeves were a tad short, but it was much warmer than his jacket.

"I hope you're not talking about me." The old man returned to his recliner. "I'd rather sit right here and watch the game." The Nuggets were ahead in the first period.

"Well, that does it then. You leave me no choice." He heaved a sigh. "Looks like I'm going to have to see if I can talk Taryn into going with me."

Gramps lifted a bushy brow. "You poor thing."

If he knew what Cash did, he'd understand what a challenge Cash was up against.

"Wish me luck," he hollered on his way out the back door.

Taryn had to stay away from Cash. That's all there was to it. Which meant she had to find someone else to help her with her business plan.

"It was a lovely wedding, don't you think?" Rose Daniels moved her latest knitting project out of the way before taking a seat in her russet swivel rocker.

"Very." Taryn unzipped her jacket and made herself at home on the soft beige sofa.

Ellie May, the Danielses' golden retriever, laid her head in Taryn's lap expecting some affection, while Jethro, a tiny Yorkie, danced on the cushion beside her.

"You guys just want some lovin', don't you?" She gave them both a vigorous rub, wishing she had brought Scout. "So, Blakely and Trent didn't have any problem with their flight?"

"Just a slight delay. I'm so glad they decided to fly out of Montrose. They deserve this time alone together."

"Yes, they do. And on the beaches of Florida, no less." Taryn glanced around the Danielses' home where Blakely and her son, Austin, lived with Rose. "Where's Austin?"

"Oh, he and Zach went over to Vinegar Hill for some sledding."

"With all this snow, I bet that place is packed today." But she was glad to learn that she and Rose were alone.

She scooted to the edge of her seat. "Rose, can I talk to you about something?"

Jethro hopped to the floor and headed for Rose.

"Of course, dear."

"And it'll stay just between you and me?"

Rose made room for the dog, a smile firmly in place. "This wouldn't have anything to do with that handsome young man you were with last night, would it?"

"You mean Cash? He's Mr. Jenkins's grandson."

"So that's his name." Rose leaned forward. "He's a hottie, all right."

"Rose, please tell me you did *not* just say that."

"Well, isn't that what you girls say about attractive men?"

"Sometimes, yes, but—"

The old woman sat back. "He sure is taken with you."

"What? No, no. Cash is attractive, I'll give you that. But he's not taken with me."

"Oh, you young people can be so blind when it comes to matters of the heart." She pulled out a good length of red yarn. "I don't believe I was ever that way. As soon as I laid eyes on Bill, I knew he was the man I was going to marry."

"How could you know that?"

Rose looked as though it was the most logical thing in the world. "Taryn, when it's right, you just know."

Taryn wished she could believe that.

She shook her head, trying to regain her original train of thought. "What I wanted to talk about is business related."

"Oh. Okay." Rose gently rocked her chair.

"Do you know anything about putting together a business plan? Like, when you apply for a business loan."

"A business loan? For what?"

"Buck's going to sell All Geared Up."

"I see." The older woman seemed to ponder the notion. "That means you'll have to give up being a guide."

"Guiding, yes. But I'll never stop climbing, Rose."

"But you're so good at being a guide. What about teaching the children at the ice festival? They so love you."

Taryn had always considered Rose one of the wisest people she knew. So she was a little taken aback by her comments. "Are you saying you don't think I should do this, Rose?"

The woman's frown turned back into a smile. She waved a hand. "Oh, I'm just thinking out loud. If God has laid this on your heart, I'm sure you'll do fine."

"So…do you know much about doing a business plan?"

"Not in the least. I'm sorry, Taryn. Bill always handled that sort of thing."

Walking back home, Taryn battled frustration and tears. *Lord, I've been all over the internet and I just don't understand this whole business plan thing. I need Your help. Please send me someone who can help me.*

She trudged through the snow, across a deserted Main Street, until she turned onto her parents' street. A block and a half later, she spotted Cash standing in their front yard.

He waved as she drew closer. "Hi." He wore an old parka that was way too small for him and he was carrying a pathetic excuse for a sled in one hand. A sled she was pretty sure had been in Mr. Jenkins's garage since before she was born.

"Hi, yourself." She burrowed her hands deeper into her pockets.

"I, uh…I was hoping to talk to you." He stopped in front of her. "About last night." His gaze bounced to the ground and back up again. "I'm sorry. I shouldn't have tried to kiss you."

His nervousness alleviated some of her anxiety. "I think

I'm the one who should apologize. I had no right to go off on you like that."

"It's obvious that I offended you."

"No, you didn't. Really. It was just—" Was she really going to tell him she thought he was somebody else? She poked at the snow with her boot. "I was tired. Not that that's any excuse. I had no right to talk to you the way I did." She squared her shoulders and dared to meet his gaze once again. "I'm sorry."

He studied her for a moment then smiled. "Make you a deal. I'll accept your apology if you'll accept mine."

The corners of her mouth twitched. "Deal."

Shifting the sled to his other hand, he held it up. "Thought I might see what kind of injury I could inflict on myself over at Vinegar Hill. Care to join me?"

"Sorry, I have something I have to take care of." She ignored the voice in her head telling her to say yes.

"Oh." His smile faltered. "Okay." He took a step back, disappointment dropping his shoulders a notch. "Well, I guess I'll catch you later then."

"See ya." She watched as he continued past her. Poor guy looked totally dejected as he wandered down the street. Head down, shoulders slumped…

She turned and started up the driveway, feeling horrible for comparing Cash to Brian. Brian never would have stopped to help those people on the mountain. Would never have apologized for offending someone. Brian didn't do anything unless it benefited him. No, Cash was definitely not Brian. Cash was a great guy.

All the more reason you should spend time with him.

She blew out a puff of air. But the more time she spent with him, the harder it would be to see him leave.

What about your business plan?

Cash knew way more about that than she ever hoped to know. *God, is Cash supposed to be the one to help me?*

Though her head didn't necessarily agree, "yes" played across her heart.

She supposed she could teach Cash a thing or two about sledding. Just not with that tiny sled he had.

The kitchen smelled like vanilla when she entered. Then she spotted the heart-shaped cookies spread across the counter. Her mom had insisted on making the cookies for Gage's daughters' Valentine's Day parties on Tuesday. Since their mother wasn't around anymore, Taryn's mom tried to help out whenever she could.

Scout trotted toward her, tail wagging.

"There you are." She scooped up her baby. "Where is everyone? Are they napping?" At this moment she was grateful for the Sunday-afternoon tradition.

She tiptoed upstairs to her room for a quick change of clothes. Ten minutes later, snow crunched under her boots, eagerness propelling each step as she towed the family toboggan behind her.

Kids of all shapes and sizes had gathered at the hill—a segment of road that was closed to traffic during the winter months. A sea of colorful ski caps stood before her. And right in the midst of them was the biggest kid of all. Not to mention the most handsome.

Cash stooped to give a child a starting push then listened as the others gave him advice on how to sled. He'd probably been here all of twenty minutes and was already the center of attention.

He goofed around and laughed with the kids, making her heart flutter all the more.

Then he saw her and the broad smile that erupted on his face wiped out any notion she had of staying away.

"Thought you were busy."

"No, I said I had something to take care of." She held her arms out to note her insulated pants and ski jacket. "I had to change clothes, silly."

"Well, you're just in time." He pointed toward the kids. "These munchkins are about to launch me on my first sled ride, and I might need somebody to notify next of kin."

"Ah, don't be such a scaredy-cat, cowboy." She infiltrated the group of kids and handed Cash the toboggan. "As big as you are, that little sled of yours—" she pointed "—won't go very far."

He assessed the hand-crafted six-footer. "Very nice."

"Do you know how to steer?"

"Not really." His cheeks and nose were as red as could be, but there was a childlike sparkle in Cash's green eyes that she found way too appealing.

"Who wants to teach him?" She scanned the kids, spotting Blakely's son and his best buddy, Zach. "Austin, think you can show Mr. Coble how it's done?"

"Sure." Austin adjusted his cap and stepped forward.

Cash paid close attention. "Got it." He started to sit on the toboggan, then paused, eyeing the kids. "I think we should talk Miss Purcell into accompanying me on my maiden flight."

"Yay!" they all cheered.

She quirked a brow, her gaze narrowing on Cash. "You're not scared, are you?"

"Not if you're with me."

The kids all chanted her name. "Taryn! Taryn! Taryn!"

"Okay. Okay." She stepped forward. "I will join you this time." She eased onto the curled-wood piece, into Cash's all-too-inviting embrace. "But you're on your own for the next run."

Snow flew for the next few hours and by the time the last remnants of daylight faded, Taryn and Cash were the only two people left at Vinegar Hill.

"I don't think I have ever laughed that much." He towed the toboggan to join her at the top of the hill.

"It's been ages since I've been over here, but this was a blast."

"I'm glad you decided to come." Beside her now, he stared down at her with that smile that was hard to resist.

But resist she must. "We should go."

"Yeah." He cast one last glance down the hill before they started up the street. "Seems every day I've been here has been a memorable one."

"Are you saying you're glad you didn't have to leave today?"

He pondered the thought, nodding his head. "I guess I am."

Snow crunched beneath their boots as they trudged along. The streets were practically abandoned. Soft light glowed from living rooms up and down the road and the aroma of burning wood hung in the air.

"What are you going to do about work?"

"I've got my laptop and phone and, thanks to you, internet. I should be able to do just about everything I do at the office. Except maybe paperwork."

"Sounds like a blessing in disguise."

"I believe you're right." He grinned. "Because now we'll have time to work on that business plan of yours."

They were in front of her house now. White covered everything in sight and lamplight spilled through the front window.

"Would you like to join Gramps and me for dinner? It's just grilled cheese and tomato soup—" he shrugged "—but they're nice and hot."

The simple combination had never sounded so good.

And Mr. Jenkins would be there. It wasn't as if they'd be alone. Not like last night. She did love spending time with the old man.

Still…

"I won't try to kiss you."

That made her laugh. "And we can discuss the whole business plan thing?"

"If you like."

She liked, all right.

"In that case, I'd love to."

Chapter Eight

Monday was almost like any other workday. Cash contacted clients and suppliers, cranked out a couple of quotes and assured his father that business was still on track. Especially now that things in the Northeast had settled and their aluminum shipment was on its way.

But, occasionally, Cash's gaze would drift past his makeshift desk in Gramps's dining room to the snow-covered landscape outside the window, reminding him just how far he was from the office. If they had snow like this in Dallas, no one would go to work, schools would be closed and the city would be virtually shut down.

Something else was different, too. Now, as the sun drifted beyond the town's western slope, he could hardly wait to call it a day and, hopefully, spend some time with Taryn.

Last night they'd only briefly discussed her business plan, meaning there was still a lot of work to be done. And they'd have to see each other to do that, right?

A smile tugged at the corners of his mouth. Any excuse to spend time with Taryn was fine by him.

Closing his laptop, he pulled his cell from his pocket

and dialed the number he'd managed to coax out of her last night.

No answer.

She was supposed to take a group climbing this morning, but he thought for sure she'd be done by now.

Instead of leaving a message, he sent her a text to call him when she got a chance.

"Something smells good, Gramps." He joined his grandfather in the kitchen. He'd heard the old man puttering around in there for the last half hour.

"Thought I'd make us some stew. Probably not as good as Taryn's, but it'll stick to your ribs."

"Are you kidding, I've always liked your stew." His cell phone beeped. Looking down at the screen, he saw a text from Taryn.

Helping Mr. Ramsey at All Geared Up. Closing at 5:30.

"Hey, Gramps, where's All Geared Up?"

"Main Street. West side, between Seventh and Eighth."

Cash checked the clock. Four forty-five. "Would you mind if I ran down there?"

Gramps swirled a wooden spoon through the pot of bubbling mixture. "Fine by me. Stew needs to simmer for a while anyway."

He donned his grandfather's coat and hat then tugged on his gloves. "I'll be back shortly."

Outside, he bypassed his rented SUV, opting to walk instead. He breathed in the chilly air, the fragrance of fresh snow and fireplaces invigorating his every step. Man, it felt good to be outside.

On the next block, a man shoveled his driveway. Cash had helped his grandfather do the same thing earlier today, adding another first to this amazing trip. He scanned the beauty around him, the mountaintops blanketed in white.

He recalled the childish notion he always had of being one with this land. Of feeling as though God lived among these magnificent mountains, tending His creation for all to see.

Maybe Gramps was right. Maybe God was keeping him here for a reason.

Traffic on Main Street was minimal. With the pass closed, there was no through traffic.

Cash strolled past shops, checking out the old buildings and window displays. Red hearts seemed to be everywhere. Then he remembered it was February. Valentine's Day. Cards, chocolate, flowers…

He shoved his hands into his pockets. Kind of lame, if you asked him. If you loved someone, shouldn't you celebrate it all the time? Not just on some fabricated holiday?

Yvette had always insisted he take her out to dinner on the few Valentine's Days they'd spent together. And he'd always done so, only more out of obligation than enthusiasm.

Spotting his destination, he crossed at the next intersection. Most of the streets had been plowed, so snow was piled high at the corners.

He eyed the display All Geared Up had in their window. Looked as if they had some pretty nice stuff. Shoving open the heavy wood-and-glass door, he stepped inside, taking in the racks of jackets and other clothing, walls of footwear and displays of climbing gear. This place was like a candy store for outdoor enthusiasts.

But he didn't see Taryn anywhere.

"May I help you?" A man Cash guessed to be in his late fifties smiled behind the U-shaped counter.

Should he say he was looking for Taryn? Nah. "I'm just looking around. Thank you."

"No problem. Let me know if you need anything."

Cash wandered through the various sections of the

store. They sure managed to get a lot of stuff into what some would consider a small space. Yet it wasn't cramped or crowded.

A black jacket caught his eye. He picked it up. Definitely more stylish than Gramps's old coat. Since he was the only one in the store, he snagged the man's attention. "Would this be suitable for ice climbing?"

"Cash?"

He jerked his head in the direction of Taryn's voice as she emerged from what appeared to be a stockroom. His pulse kicked up a notch.

"Hey, there." He couldn't help smiling. He really was glad to see her.

"What are you doing here?" She moved toward him.

"Thought I'd check things out." He held the jacket in front of him. "What do you think?"

She nodded. "Looks good."

"Would it be suitable for ice climbing?"

Her brow lifted. "When are you planning to climb?"

"I don't know. But if the opportunity should present itself, I'd like to be prepared."

"I see." Humor danced in her pale blue eyes. "Well, then—" She took a step closer, retrieved a second jacket in navy blue. "That one is good, but this one would probably be better. Just as warm but with a little less bulk."

He liked the sound of that. Depositing his selection back on the rack, he shrugged out of his grandfather's parka. "Mind holding this?"

She draped it over her arm as he took her recommendation off the hanger.

"Feels lighter."

"A little bit. Yes."

He slipped it on. "Very comfortable."

"It's one of our most popular brands."

"Well, you folks certainly know more about winter

clothing than I do." He stepped in front of a nearby mirror. Looked as good as it felt.

Taryn peered around him. "That's a good color for you."

Her approval did strange things to him. But even if she hadn't said anything, he was sold. "I'll take it."

"Boy, you're easy."

"Not really." He removed the coat, his gaze fixed on Taryn's. "I simply found what I was looking for."

Taryn wasn't sure whether to run away or melt into a puddle right there. The way Cash looked at her...

The phone rang behind the counter, bringing her back to her senses. She took the coat and headed for the cash register. How stupid. She would never be exactly what anyone was looking for.

"What about a hat?"

She dared to turn around.

Cash grabbed a matching blue knit hat from atop one of the racks. "This a good one?"

"Sure is." Turning on her heel, she continued behind the counter.

"I'll be in the backroom if you need me." Buck was already halfway there, phone to his ear.

"Oh." Did she dare say that she needed him so she wouldn't be alone with Cash? "Okay."

"And you can go ahead and leave when you're done." With that, Buck disappeared behind the curtain.

Cash stepped to the counter. "Looks like you get to go home."

"Uh-huh." She nodded, scanning the bar codes on his purchases.

"Did you walk or drive today?" He pulled a credit card from his wallet.

Taryn was afraid of where this conversation was headed. "Drove. How about you?"

"I walked."

Wonderful. Now he probably expected her to ask if he wanted a ride. Which she would if he were anybody else. But he wasn't anybody. He was Cash Coble. Tall, kind-hearted, sweet Texan who seemed to know just how to worm his way into her heart.

Guilt nudged as she told Cash his total and swiped his card. She was the one with the problem, not Cash. "Would...you like a ride home?"

"That'd be great. Thanks."

"There's something I meant to ask you," he said as he climbed into her Jeep a few minutes later. "What would you think about getting together tonight, after dinner, to go over your business plan? After talking to you last night, I came up with some ideas and thought maybe we could discuss them over coffee at that Mouse's Chocolate and Coffee place."

She shifted her Jeep into Reverse, a battle raging inside her head. She knew she needed to avoid Cash, but at the same time, he was the only one who seemed to know anything about business plans. And she needed that business plan. Then again, Mouse's wasn't exactly an intimate environment. And this was strictly business. Wasn't it?

"Sounds good. And it'll give me an excuse to have one of their scraps cookies." She started to drive up the street.

"What's that?"

"You mean, besides the most amazing thing you've ever put in your mouth?" She laughed, making a left at the Beaumont Hotel. "The cookie dough is some family recipe, but just kind of a basic dough. Then they add whatever scraps they have left over from the chocolate they made that day."

"Really?"

"Yep. No two cookies are the same. You might get one with bits of toffee or chocolate bark or who knows what."

"You must really like these cookies."

"They're my favorite." She turned right. "Which is why I don't allow myself to indulge very often. Even then, it's only one."

She pulled up to her parents' house.

"Guess I'll have to try one, then." Cash smiled from the passenger side.

"I warn you. They're addictive. And you can't get them anywhere else."

"Hmm…" He opened his door. "Seems there are a lot of things like that in Ouray."

She hopped down from the Jeep into the snow. Why did he keep saying stuff like that? Refusing to look behind her, she continued up the steps. "I'll meet you there at seven."

Cash was waiting when Taryn arrived at Mouse's at two minutes after seven. Then again, he'd left the house at six forty-five and driven his rental the entire three blocks, something he decided was completely stupid. The vehicle didn't even have a chance to warm up.

But Taryn had said to meet her—not walk or ride with her.

He stood from the booth where he'd set up his laptop.

Her smile was tentative, as though she was nervous. But why?

She tugged at the deep purple scarf around her neck. "Have you ordered yet?"

"No." He shoved his hands into his pockets. "I was waiting for you." A feat he found nearly impossible with the incredible aromas of coffee and chocolate wafting around him.

"You shouldn't have done that." No smile this time. Almost as though she was scolding him.

"I was getting things set up." He gestured to his computer.

"Oh." Her gaze fell to her feet. "Well, shall we then?" She started toward the counter.

A man close to Cash's age stepped up to the other side. "What's up, Taryn?"

"Not much. How's things with you, Jeb?"

"Can't complain. What can I get you?"

"I'll have a hot chocolate."

He glanced at Cash. "You two together?"

"Yes," said Cash before Taryn could say anything to the contrary. "I'll have a caramel latte." He eyed the glass case filled with all sorts of chocolate creations.

"You're a better person than I am." Taryn shook her head. "That'd keep me awake half the night."

He was used to the caffeine when he worked late nights at home. But late nights were not the norm at Gramps's. "You know, you're right." He eyed Jeb. "Make mine a hot chocolate, too."

"Oh, and two—" Taryn's gaze drifted to Cash's "—scraps cookies?"

"Yes. Two, please."

Cardboard-sleeved cups in hand, they retreated to the Formica-covered booth and shed their coats. Cash inspected his cookie, which looked different from Taryn's, even though they were both scraps cookies. Bits of chocolate, nuts and other goodies littered his. "This looks amazing."

"Trust me, it is." Her eyes closed as she savored her first bite.

He took a bite, too. "Mmm…" He continued to chew. Then stared at the cookie again. "Caramel and chocolate."

"It's not a science experiment, Cash. Just enjoy it."

He grinned. Then took a second bite and chased it with a sip of hot chocolate. "Whoa!" He stared at the cup.

"Too hot?"

"I've never tasted hot chocolate like that before. That's amazing."

She smiled. "Their secret recipe."

"Glad I followed your lead."

Cookie devoured, he dusted off his hands and pulled up the file he'd created for Taryn's project on his computer.

"So what did you think about All Geared Up?"

"It's great. And you obviously know your stuff." He lifted his new jacket. "Keeps me toasty warm."

That earned him another smile.

"Good." Taryn opened the notebook she'd brought. "I wrote out my mission statement, vision statement and the company background. Of course, those were the easy parts."

"But they're still things you need, so good job." He turned the laptop so she could see the screen.

"When I was there today, I tried to get a better feel for the assets."

"Did you include the apartments upstairs?"

"Yes."

"And the furnishings, since Buck plans on leaving those."

"Good, good." He scrolled through the document. "As far as competitor analysis, there really aren't any in town that I can tell."

"No. There are a few outfitters in Telluride and Montrose, but that's about it."

"Okay. Now let's talk about the financial portion of this." The door opened again, bringing with it another blast of cold air. This place was busier than he expected.

"Ugh. I don't even—"

"What has you two so deep in conversation?"

Cash and Taryn both looked up to see Taryn's brother, Randy, standing beside them.

"Nothing that concerns you, big brother."

Following Taryn's cue, Cash closed his laptop. "Good to see you again, buddy." He stood to shake his friend's hand.

"I heard you got held over."

He shrugged. "Can't do much about the weather."

"What are you doing here?" Taryn eyed her brother.

"Just looking."

She lifted a brow. "Yeah, right." She got up from her seat. "My guess is you forgot to get something for Amanda for Valentine's Day."

Guilt clouded Randy's features. "Maybe."

"Don't you dare let me catch you giving her one of those prepackaged boxes they have. You can at least have the courtesy to put together a box with all of her favorites."

"Favorites?" Randy chuckled. "She likes everything they have."

"There you go, then. Get her one of everything." Taryn sent him a mischievous grin.

"Yeah, yeah, yeah." Randy glanced behind him as two more last-minute shoppers wandered in. "I'd better get in line. I'll talk to you two later."

Cash and Taryn slid back into the booth.

"Kinda reminded me of me and my sister," said Cash.

"Megan, right?"

"Yeah."

"How is she?" Taryn folded her hands on the table.

"At the moment, very pregnant. She's expecting twins."

"Oh, wow. And she already has one child, correct?"

"A girl, yes."

"Sounds like she's going to have her hands full."

"Yes, she will." He opened his laptop again. "Now, about that financial statement—"

His cell phone rang and he tugged it from his pocket with a groan. "It's my father. Sorry. I'd better take this."

Taryn had really hoped to make a dent in her business plan, but it didn't appear that was going to happen tonight. Too many interruptions. First Randy, then Cash's dad.

As Cash's telephone conversation with his father wore on, she quietly excused herself and went to help her brother, who, even from across the room, looked totally perplexed.

"Need some help?" She bumped Randy with her elbow as she joined him at the expansive glass case.

"I've got all her favorite truffles, I'm just trying to decide what else to get."

"Well, how about some toffee or Turtles? She likes nuts, doesn't she?"

"Yeah. Good idea." He completed his order and waited while they wrapped the box. "So what's going on with you and Cash?"

"Nothing romantic, if that's what you're thinking."

Her brother grinned down at her. "Nah, that's Mom's job."

Turning, she watched Cash. His body language had changed.

"Whoever he's talking to, he doesn't look happy," said Randy.

Tension knitted Cash's brow. His shoulders had grown stiff.

She folded her arms across her chest. "It's his father."

Images of a genuinely happy Cash flashed through her mind. When she took him climbing, and the other day sledding at Vinegar Hill. That's the Cash she liked to see. The one she was trying desperately not to fall for. And the one she'd like to see at least one more time before he returned to Dallas.

"All right, sis." Randy paid his bill and grabbed the beautifully wrapped package. "I'm out of here." He gave her a hug and kissed the top of her head, something he'd done since she was a kid.

She hugged him back. "See ya."

As the door closed behind Randy, she returned to her seat.

"I got it. All right, Dad. We'll talk tomorrow." Cash ended the call. "I am so sorry about that."

"Problem?"

"Not really. But he seems to think so."

"Sounds like you're also chief executive of talk-'em-down-from-the-ledge." That made him smile, which she was glad to see.

"Yeah, where Dad's concerned, I seem to be wearing that hat more and more often. Especially with my mom gone to be with Megan."

"So that's usually her role?"

He shrugged. "They've been married for thirty-five years. She's had a lot of practice."

"I know what you mean." She leaned forward, resting her forearms on the table. "Dad's that way with my mom. They complement each other. Where one is weak, the other is strong."

"Sounds like a good basis for marriage."

"I've always thought so." She glanced around to see they were the only ones left in the store and workers had started putting things away. "Looks like they're getting ready to close."

"I was afraid of that." He clicked a few keys then closed his laptop. "I'm sorry I wasted your time."

"What? No, you didn't waste my time. I don't suppose you could break away for a few hours tomorrow, though, could you?"

"To work on your business plan?"

"No, to go climbing. Thought I might take you over to the ice park."

"Really?"

She had to laugh when his face lit up like a child's. "Yes, really. You had so much fun the first time. Plus, you've got that new jacket we need to break in."

He glanced down at his coat. "You're right, we do."

"So, what works best for you? Morning or afternoon?"

"How about somewhere in between. Say, ten-thirty?"

"It's a date."

Chapter Nine

Today was the perfect day for ice climbing. Temps were in the twenties and the sun was as bright as it could be. Taryn had to admit she was actually looking forward to climbing with Cash today. She wanted him to relax and have fun. Those dimples of his would simply be a bonus.

She loaded their gear into her Jeep then headed next door to get Cash. Birds that had been taking advantage of Mr. Jenkins's feeder took flight as she passed.

Hopefully, Cash had taken care of whatever work his father was so concerned about last night. She didn't want anything hanging over his head today. Except lots of ice.

Smiling, she knocked on the front door.

Mr. Jenkins opened it. He was wearing her favorite flannel shirt, a green-and-blue plaid that looked great with his green eyes. "Mornin', Taryn." He held the door wide, inviting her inside.

Flames flickered inside the fireplace.

"Is Cash ready?" She heard his voice then. Could see him pacing in the kitchen, phone to his ear.

The old man frowned, closing the door behind her. "He's been on that thing since before sunup."

That didn't bode well. "Is something wrong?"

"I'm afraid so."

Cash's gaze met hers and the look on his face was one of pure anguish. Her heart tightened. They were not going climbing.

"I'll call you back, Dad." He pocketed the phone and strode across the tan carpet, rubbing the back of his neck. "Gramps, would you excuse us for a minute, please?"

The old man nodded. "Need to get back to my laundry anyway."

As his grandfather disappeared into the kitchen, Cash turned her to look at him. "I'm sorry, I should have called you. I didn't realize how late it was." Stubble lined his usually clean-shaven jaw and pain had settled into his eyes.

"What's wrong?"

"There was a fire at the plant last night."

Her eyes widened. "Is everyone all right?"

"Yeah. No one was there except a security guard."

"I hope he caught it early." She searched his weary gaze, looking for answers.

"Relatively. It was confined to one area. Still…"

A sudden chill filled the air, despite the logs crackling in the fireplace. Oh, how she ached for him. If only there was something she could do.

"Your father must be beside himself."

He raked his fingers through his already mussed blond hair. "That's an understatement. I've been talking with him, our foreman and the insurance company all morning."

"That's what your grandfather said."

His hand cupped her cheek. "I was *really* looking forward to climbing with you today." He wasn't the only one. But there was no way she could tell him that. That would only make him feel worse.

"Stuff happens." She clasped her hand around his and

lowered it. Gave a reassuring squeeze. "I understand. Your dad needs you."

"Yeah." His gaze fell.

She ducked to meet it. "Hey, I'm here if you need me, okay?"

"Okay." One corner of his mouth lifted. A halfhearted smile if she'd ever seen one.

"I'd better go so you can get back to your dad." She started to turn, but he tugged her back, refusing to let go.

"Let me take you to dinner tonight."

"It's Valentine's Day, Cash. Getting a table might be a bit of a challenge."

"I don't care if I have to wait all night." He squeezed tighter. "Please?" There was an urgency in his tone.

How could she refuse when he looked so miserable? "Sure. Just let me know when you want to go."

"Okay." His efforts at a smile were a little better this time. "I'll call you later."

Taryn couldn't deny her disappointment as she trudged through the packed snow, back to her parents' house. More than anything, she wanted to see Cash happy. Instead, he was worse than ever. And it broke her heart.

Rumors had been swirling around town that the pass might be reopened later today. If that was the case, Cash would leave tomorrow. And while her head told her that was a good thing, her heart wasn't ready to see him go.

Cash knocked on the Purcells' front door. The prospect of spending time with Taryn had been a bright spot in an otherwise gloomy day. And he hoped beyond hope that, before the end of the evening, he could talk her into pursuing a long-distance relationship. Sure, it wasn't ideal, but he had to try. He'd be a fool to let a woman as amazing as Taryn go without a fight.

He heard Scout barking inside.

When Taryn opened the door and the dog recognized him, Scout's entire body wiggled, right along with her tail. She bounced up and down against his leg.

"Well, hey there, Miss Scout." He picked her up. Stroked the shock of white fur under her chin. She caught his face between her front paws, one on each cheek, and licked his chin.

"Scout, you silly girl." Taryn rescued him by taking the dog. "Sorry about that. In case you can't tell, she really likes you."

"That's good." He wiped his face. "Because I kind of like her, too." *Right along with her owner.*

He got a good look at Taryn then and his pulse kicked up a notch. She wore a silky blue blouse that really brought out her eyes. Skinny jeans were tucked into a pair of fur-lined boots, revealing long, slender legs.

"You have to stay here with Grandma and Grandpa," Taryn said to the dog. She was a born nurturer. The kind that would make a great mom.

"Taryn, honey, don't make Cash wait outside. It's cold out there." Her mother appeared behind her.

"No worries, Bonnie. We're leaving anyway."

Taryn donned her coat.

"So where are you two going?" Her mother's eyes were alight with pleasure.

"I'm not sure yet. Figured I'd let Taryn pick, or we'll just see what strikes our fancy." He offered his arm to Taryn. "Ready?"

She tugged her purple beanie. "Ready." She slipped a gloved hand in the crook of his elbow. "See you later, Mom."

"Have a good time."

"How are things at the factory?" Taryn asked before they made their way to the sidewalk.

"A little better, I suppose." He laid his gloved hand atop

hers, liking the way it felt. "Though to hear my dad, it's the end of the world."

"I'm sorry. I know this is hard on you."

"Ah, I'm used to it." Rounding the corner, he was ready to talk about anything but work. "So what did you do today?"

"My boss over at Marmot Mountain Guides called shortly after I left you. One of the other guides was sick, so I ended up taking his group." She paused suddenly. "I hope you're not mad."

"Why would I be mad?" He smiled at her. "Disappointed that I wasn't the one climbing with you, maybe. But not mad."

"I know you really wanted to go climbing."

"Yeah, I really did."

Snow crunched under their feet and their breath filled the air.

"I heard they reopened the pass this afternoon."

"Yep. I'm already booked on the afternoon flight tomorrow." Not that he was exactly thrilled about it. He wanted more time in Ouray. More time with Taryn.

"Guess they got it open just in time." Her smile faltered, making him wonder if she'd be sad to see him leave. He was certainly going to miss her.

"I don't know." He continued to hold her hand in place. "I wouldn't have minded a couple of more days."

"You can always come back, you know." Her expectant look gave him hope.

"I know." If his dad would ever let him leave again. They turned onto Main Street at the Beaumont Hotel. "So what are you hungry for?"

"How do you feel about Mexican?"

"You're kidding, right? I'm from Texas. I was weaned on Mexican food."

Her smile was bright. "Good. Then why don't we see if we can get in at Buen Tiempo."

The restaurant was packed, but they decided to wait for a table, and he was glad they did.

"Those were some of the best enchiladas I've ever had," he said as the waitress cleared their dishes. He leaned back in his seat and scanned the bustling restaurant.

"Just wait 'til you try their chocolate cake." Taryn grinned across the wooden table.

"Why are there dollar bills stuck to the ceiling?"

She glanced upward. "Just something they do for fun. People get a kick out of it and give their servers bills to tack up there." She lowered her gaze. "Then, once a year or so, they take what's up there and donate it to charity."

"That's cool." If they weren't so busy, he'd consider joining in the fun. But he was on a mission.

As time stretched on, he found himself growing more and more nervous. He had yet to tell Taryn how he felt about her. Kind of tough for someone who wasn't used to talking about their feelings. However, he'd never met a woman like her. And he didn't want to let this moment slip away.

He retrieved a small box from his jacket pocket and slid it across the table. "Happy Valentine's Day."

"Wha—? For me?" Taryn's eyes were huge. Her smile evaporated and she pushed the box back. "N-no. I can't."

Flashbacks of Brian and the gifts he gave her rushed through Taryn's mind. Gifts he would use to manipulate her.

She pushed the horrid thoughts away and focused on the man across the table. Taryn didn't want to hurt Cash's feelings, but there was no way she could accept what was inside that long, narrow velvet box. Jewelry came in boxes like that. Why would he give her jewelry, though?

"Taryn, please. It's okay. It's not what you think."

He knew what she was thinking? How embarrassing.

Taking hold of the package, she slid off the shiny gold ribbon and, after a quick glance at his expectant gaze, she opened it. "A flash drive?"

"No, not just a flash drive. It's your business plan."

"My…" Emotion clogged her throat.

"I know you've been eager to get it done. And since our meeting last night never really got off the ground, well… I worked on it when I got home. There are some numbers you'll need to plug in on the financial statements, and you may want to tweak some of my wording, but it's all there."

"You did this for me?" Tears welled in her eyes, but she blinked them away. She couldn't remember the last time someone had done something that meant so much. And the fact that it was Cash made her frozen heart melt just a little more.

"Taryn—" He leaned forward.

"One slice of chocolate cake." The waitress plunked the plate in the middle of the table. "And two forks." She set them beside the plate.

"Thank you," said Cash before the woman scurried away. "This looks amazing."

They devoured the dessert in record time, though Taryn was pretty sure she ate more than half.

Cash paid the bill and helped her with her coat. Outside, the clear sky had given way to a multitude of stars.

"Thank you again," she said as they walked up the street. "Not just for dinner, but for the business plan." Her fingers clasped the box inside her pocket.

"It's important to you." He stopped as they rounded the corner. "And *you're* important to me."

Her heart took a nosedive. He was going there. The one place she didn't want to—no, couldn't—go. She met his gaze. "Cash—"

"Look, I know you live here and I live in Dallas. But I also know that it's easier for people to stay in touch than ever before. We can talk, FaceTime, Skype every day." He took hold of her free hand. "You're the most incredible woman I've ever met, Taryn. I just want to get to know you better."

"And then what?" She couldn't go into a relationship without coming clean about her past. What would Cash think when he learned not only about the baby but about Brian?

"I don't know. I guess we'll play it by ear."

Taryn's heart stopped. Once he got an earful of her past, he'd be looking for a way to be rid of her. She was sure of that.

She shook her head. "It'll never work, Cash. There are things about me you don't want to know. Trust me, you deserve better."

He puffed out a disbelieving laugh that hung in the air between them. "Well, that sounds like a cop-out."

"I'm not copping out. Just being realistic." She started walking again, suddenly eager to get home.

"What are you so afraid of?" He caught up to her in two strides.

"Cash, I'm sorry if I made you believe I wanted anything more than friendship. But I'm just not relationship material."

Grabbing hold of her elbow, he turned her to face him. Her own pain and hurt reflected in Cash's eyes, yet he stared at her for what seemed like forever. And try as she might, she couldn't look away.

"Some guy really did a number on you, didn't he? And I'm guessing he was from Texas."

She opened her mouth to speak but closed it without saying a word. What could she say without going into the ugly details?

Cash's gaze darkened then narrowed. "So you think *I'm* like this other guy?" He looked away, shaking his head in disbelief. "Thanks for the vote of confidence." He faced her again. "Well, here's a news flash. I'm *not* him. But, if that's what you believe, then I guess you're right. It would never work between us."

She couldn't blame him for being angry. And though she didn't like it, she supposed it was better than letting him think they stood a chance.

He touched her elbow. "Time to go home."

The next morning, Cash pushed himself away from the kitchen table. "Thanks for breakfast, Gramps."

"My pleasure, son." The old man patted him on the back. "I'm going to miss you."

"Me, too." There were a lot of things he was going to miss. He set his dishes in the sink. "I need to finish packing and grab a shave."

He took the steps two at a time. While a part of him was eager to get back to Dallas, another part wished he could stay and smooth things out with Taryn. After an otherwise wonderful night, he'd let anger, perhaps pride, get the best of him.

Why had he brought up the subject of a relationship anyway? Hadn't she already said she had no desire to return to Texas? And it wasn't as if he could move to Ouray.

In the small bathroom, he splashed a handful of warm water over his face then looked in the mirror.

Misery stared back at him. Perhaps it had always been there and he simply couldn't put a name to it. But then, he'd never been so torn between duty to his father and chasing his own dreams. At least not since he first took over the company.

God, I don't know what to do.

Another desperate prayer. He knew God wanted more from him. So why did he refuse to give it?

Time.

Prayer took time. Time was always of the essence. Or so he thought. But shouldn't God be at the essence of everything he did?

He tossed his shaving kit into his suitcase as he entered the bedroom then dropped onto the bed. *God, I thought, maybe, Taryn was part of the reason You brought me to Ouray. She's going to be hard to forget.*

She brought out the man he used to be. A man who hadn't seen the light of day in a long time. Too long.

Standing, he gathered the rest of his belongings, zipped his suitcase and carried it downstairs.

"Gramps?" He set his bag by the door then went into the kitchen. "Hmph. Wonder where he went."

He moved to the old dining table to pack up his laptop. Movement outside the window caught his eye.

Saw in hand, his grandfather climbed an eight-foot ladder he'd positioned beneath the pine tree by the driveway. The one whose snow-laden limbs had draped over the driveway and scraped against the house. The one Cash had promised to trim.

He rushed out the front door and around the side of the house. "Gramps! No!"

The old man reached for the limb with his free hand. The ladder wobbled.

Horror pulsed through Cash's veins as the ladder went one way and Gramps tumbled helplessly the other.

Knees in the air, Gramps was still on his back when Cash dropped beside him.

"Gramps! Are you okay?" Dread seeped into Cash's bones.

"My back." His grandfather rolled onto all fours with a

groan, his breath visible in the frigid morning air. "Help me into the house."

"Are you sure? Maybe I should call an ambulance."

"And leave me in the snow?" The old man held up a hand. "Just. Get me. To the house."

Cash gripped his grandfather's arm and helped him to his feet.

Hunched over, Gramps could hardly walk. Pain was etched all over his face.

And it was all Cash's fault.

He eased his grandfather up the steps, his heart clenched with grief. If anything happened to Gramps...

Inside, the old man tried to sit in his recliner but opted for the couch. He lay on his back, knees again in the air, though nothing seemed to relieve the pain.

Sweat beaded Cash's brow. He didn't know what to do.

Taryn was the only person he could think to call. But after last night, would she even answer the phone?

Pulling out his cell, he punched in her number and ducked into the kitchen.

It took three rings, but at least she answered.

"Taryn. Gramps fell. Off the ladder. He hurt his back and I...I don't know what to do."

"Where is he now?"

"In the living room."

"I'm on my way."

By the time Cash rejoined his grandfather, Taryn was sprinting across the yard. He met her at the door.

She glanced at him briefly before moving on to Gramps. "Mr. Jenkins." She knelt at his side. "Tell me where it hurts." Compassion filled her voice.

"My...my back." He winced. "Hit my...tailbone."

Standing, she looked at Cash, nodded toward the kitchen then started that way.

He followed, his gut churning as he glanced back at Gramps.

Once inside, she said, "He's not going to like it, but we need to get the EMTs over here. He'll need an X-ray, but I don't want to risk moving him ourselves."

"I'm with you one hundred percent."

Her questioning gaze met his. "What about your flight?"

For a moment he'd forgotten about getting back to Dallas. But did she really think he would leave when Gramps was hurt?

"Forget about my flight. I'm not going anywhere until I know he's okay."

Chapter Ten

Taryn had really hoped to get to the bank this morning. She still couldn't believe Cash had put together that entire business plan for her. And he'd done an amazing job. She'd gotten up early to make what few changes needed to be made, then she'd planned to print out the document and drop her entire package off with Cam at the bank later today.

But that was before Cash's grandfather fell. Now she followed the ambulance to Montrose Memorial Hospital. Mr. Jenkins was more important than any business venture. She had to know how he was doing.

Cash had opted to ride in the ambulance. And who could blame him? After the way she treated him last night, she was surprised he'd called her. Then again, it wasn't like he had many options. She was the only person in town he really knew.

Except he didn't really know her, did he? Nobody but Blakely did.

Boy, could she use her friend's input right now. On second thought…she never held back when it came to Blakely. When Trent came back into her life, Taryn had pushed and prodded, wanting her friend to see the big picture. And Blakely would likely do the same to her.

Yep, it was a good thing that Blakely was on a beach somewhere in Florida with her husband, instead of pointing Taryn in directions she really didn't want to go. She didn't deserve a man like Cash.

Both hands on the steering wheel, she continued north on Highway 550 as fast as she dared.

Some guy really did a number on you. How had Cash figured that out? She'd spent most of the night pondering that and still didn't have any answers.

She shrugged off the memory as Montrose Memorial came into view. She snagged the first parking place she could find and hurried to meet the ambulance.

The EMTs had put a neck brace on Mr. Jenkins before transferring him to a backboard. Something he was even less happy about than the ambulance. At least he seemed to listen to her when she explained why it was necessary.

She really loved that old man.

Cash was right beside the gurney as they wheeled his grandfather through the automatic doors, past the waiting area and straight to an examination room.

Taryn paused at the doors that divided the waiting room from the treatment area. As much as she would have liked to go with them, she felt it wasn't her place. She wasn't family.

The doors were almost shut, when they suddenly opened again.

Cash took a step toward her. "Aren't you coming?"

Her heart swelled. Whether he wanted her there or simply understood how much she cared, she didn't know. But he needed her, despite the way she'd rejected, perhaps even hurt, him last night. For that, she was grateful.

Antiseptic smells drifted around her as she followed Cash down the long hallway. Inside the small triage unit, the EMTs relayed the necessary information to the hospital medical team.

"Mr. Jenkins, on a scale of one to ten, ten being the worst, what's your level of pain?" A nurse checked the old man's IV line.

"Nine."

"Do you have any allergies?" A second nurse tore open a syringe packet.

"No." The old man's voice was raspy.

Standing in the corner of the room, Cash watched the frenzy of activity, looking like a scared little boy.

Taryn closed the space that separated them, slipped her hand in the crook of his arm and gave it a squeeze.

He looked at her hand first then her face. He smiled, tentative, but enough to let her know he was glad for the support.

Shoes squeaked against the polished floor as hospital personnel moved in and out of the room.

A thin, dark-haired man approached them. "I assume you're family."

"I'm his grandson." Cash motioned to Taryn. "She's a close family friend."

"We'll need to do an MRI." The doctor addressed both of them. "You're welcome to accompany him."

"We'd like that." Cash laid his hand atop hers, a move she refused to analyze right now. "Thank you."

A short time later, they sat quietly in the radiology waiting room.

"This is my fault." Cash pushed out of the brown upholstered chair and ran a hand over his face.

"Don't be so hard on yourself. Your grandfather's doing stuff like that all the time. When he sees something that needs to be done, he does it."

"But I was supposed to do it." He whirled toward her, his face red. "When it snowed the other day, he said he didn't like the way the branch scraped against the house. I promised him I'd take care of it." Dropping back into his chair, he leaned his head against the wall. "But I didn't."

The pain in his eyes was almost palpable. How she wished she could take it away.

"Cash, I can guarantee you that your grandfather does not blame you for what happened."

"You're right. That's not his way." He looked at her now. "But *I* blame me."

She met Cash's tender gaze. "I don't think your grandfather would want you to do that. You know there's this wonderful thing called forgiveness, right?"

"Yes. But sometimes it's easier to forgive others than it is to forgive ourselves."

Leaning back in her chair, she blew out a breath. "Don't I know it." She'd had plenty of practice.

"I'm preaching to the choir, huh?" The corners of his mouth lifted. "So what have you done that's so unforgivable?"

Cash watched Taryn's face change. Her smile faltered. Her eyes lost their spark. His question had obviously struck a nerve. But why?

She pushed to her feet. "I could really use a cup of coffee. Can I get you anything?" Her forced smile did little to hide whatever turmoil was going on inside.

"Coffee would be great."

"Good." She disappeared through the door, leaving him alone in the otherwise empty room.

He recalled their post-dinner conversation last night. She'd said there were things about her he wouldn't want to know. That he deserved better. At the time, he thought she was just trying to let him down easy. But now?

He stared at the door. Something haunted her, all right. And he'd bet it had to do with a guy. Perhaps the one he'd alluded to last night. And he couldn't help thinking that it had something to do with her time in Texas.

So many questions. Yet they did little to diminish his feelings for her. Feelings that seemed to grow stronger every time they were together.

His phone vibrated in his pocket. He pulled it out and looked at the screen. *Dad.*

May as well get it over with. "Hello."

"Glad you finally decided to answer."

"What?" He wasn't in the mood for his father's interrogation.

"I've been trying to call you. Have you made it to the airport yet?"

This was not going to go over well. Though, at this point, he didn't really care. "No, and it doesn't look like I'm going to, either."

"What are you talking about?"

He let go a frustrated sigh. "I'm at the hospital, Dad. Gramps fell off a ladder and hurt his back. They're doing an MRI on him now."

"He shouldn't be getting on a ladder at his age."

Pour salt in the wound, why don't you. "I know that. But then, he's not your typical ninety-year-old, either." He stood and paced the small space.

"I'll give you that." His father chuckled. "Hope I'm in as good shape when I'm his age." He paused. "Have you told your mother yet?"

Cash dreaded the thought. The woman was a worrywart when it came to her father. "No. I wanted to wait until I knew the extent of his injury."

"That's probably best."

"Yep." But was his dad still going to demand he come back?

"Well, we'll hire a nurse to care for him once his injuries are determined, then we'll get you on a plane right away. Tomorrow, if possible."

"What? Are you crazy? There's no way I'm leaving tomorrow."

Silence filtered through the line.

"Come on, Dad. Be reasonable. What would Mom say if I left in such a hurry?"

"Yeah, I reckon you're right. We can wait 'til this weekend."

Cash heaved out a sigh. The man was exasperating. "I can't talk right now. I'll call you later." He buried the phone in his pocket. There was no way Cash was going to let the man pressure him into coming back any sooner than necessary.

The door opened and Taryn breezed in with two cardboard-sleeved cups. "I got you a caramel latte." Her usually bubbly disposition seemed to have returned.

Rubbing the back of his neck with one hand, he accepted the drink with the other. "Thank you."

She studied him a moment. "Are you okay?"

"Not really." He dropped into his chair. "My dad just called."

"I see." She settled beside him once again. "What did he say?"

"He's still expecting me to come back right away. And get this. He wants to hire someone to take care of Gramps."

"Well…" She tucked her hair behind her ear. "What are your plans for going back?"

"I don't know." He raked a hand through his hair. "At this point, I'm going to have to wait and see." He took a sip. "Mmm… This is good."

She smiled. "I remembered you ordering a caramel latte at Mouse's the other night, so I took a chance."

"Well, I'm glad you did." Before he could second-guess

the move, he clasped her free hand in his. "Thank you for being here."

She looked at him, her expression earnest. "Your grandfather is very important to me."

"And what about me? Am I important to you?" He sensed her trying to pull away, but he held fast.

She took a deep breath. Met his gaze. "Yes. I just wish things were simpler."

"Mr. Coble?"

He looked at the technician across the room.

Rotten timing.

"Your grandfather did great. If you'd like to follow me, we'll be moving him to a temporary room."

The aroma of dinner lingered in the air as Cash paced the hallway outside his grandfather's room. For hospital food, that roast beef Gramps had sure looked good. Cash's stomach growled now; the sandwich Taryn had brought him for lunch was a distant memory.

"He has a broken back, Mom." He pressed the phone against his ear. "A compression fracture."

"Oh, no. Is he going to need surgery?"

"No." Surgery would be rough on someone Gramps's age. "He'll have to wear a specially made brace for several weeks, though."

"Bless his heart, he's not going to like that."

"Probably not. But it beats the alternative." *Of course, if you had taken care of the branch in the first place, like you promised, Gramps wouldn't be here at all.*

"Poor Dad."

A woman wearing brightly colored scrubs smiled as she moved past him, pushing one of those carts they use to check blood pressure and such.

He leaned against the handrail. "They said if everything

goes okay, he can go home on Friday. But even then, he's not going to be able to live by himself for a while."

"Oh, Cash." Distress laced his mother's tone. "I don't know what to do. Megan could deliver any day and there's no one else who can stay with Annie Grace."

"Mom, it's okay. I wasn't asking you to come." He knew she needed to be there for his niece.

"Well…what are you going to do then?"

Air whirred through the ventilation system overhead.

"It's my fault he fell, so I plan to stay here until he's well enough to be on his own again." A decision he'd made shortly before Taryn left.

"Your fault? How can it be your fault?"

He briefly explained.

"Oh, Cash."

"Dad's not going to be too thrilled about my decision, but between my phone and my laptop, I can work just as easily from here."

"Don't you worry about your father. I can handle him. We're all having to make sacrifices. He's just going to have to deal with it."

Cash couldn't help laughing. "I'd like to be a fly on the wall during that conversation."

"Oh, stop. Now, let me talk to your grandfather. That is, if he's feeling up to it."

Cash stepped back into the room.

Gramps fiddled with the controls on the bed. The poor guy had yet to find a comfortable position.

"He's a little groggy from pain meds, but his spirits are good." Cash caught his grandfather's eye. "Mom wants to talk to you." He passed off the phone and pulled up a chair while they chatted.

"They're all making a fuss over me." Gramps paused and listened. "Well, I don't like it. Not one bit." He paused again. "All right. Bye-bye."

He handed the phone back to Cash. "Don't you think it's about time for you to head on home?"

"Nope. I'm staying here with you."

His grandfather's brow furrowed. "You don't have to do that."

"What, and miss out on a chance to sleep on that fold-out vinyl bed?" He gestured to the beige chair in the corner. "Besides, I don't have a car. I rode in the ambulance with you, remember?"

"You could have gone home with Taryn."

"I didn't want to go home with Taryn. I want to stay here with you. However, I'm starting to get the impression you don't want me here."

The old man frowned. "Of course, I do, son. I just don't like putting you out. You've already been here longer than you planned. You should be back in Dallas."

He leaned closer. "Gramps, I can't leave you." Emotion filled his throat. He reached for his grandfather's wrinkled hand lying atop the white blanket. "I'm sorry I didn't take care of that branch. I said I would and…I let you down."

The old man's grip tightened as a hint of a smile formed. "Cash, you could never let me down."

Suddenly, Cash felt like a little boy again. Tears stung the backs of his eyes. He blinked them away. "Can you ever forgive me?"

"There's nothing to forgive. I told you before, son, I don't believe in coincidence. God has a reason for everything. We should just be thankful it wasn't as bad as it could have been."

Cash sniffed. He was beyond thankful.

Standing, he smoothed Gramps's blanket and repositioned his pillows. "But for the foreseeable future, you're stuck with me. Because this is exactly where I want to be."

Chapter Eleven

What was wrong with her?

Taryn had lost more sleep since Cash arrived in Ouray than ever before. And saying goodbye seemed to get more difficult every time. Yet she kept going back for more, even when she knew she'd end up with a broken heart.

With Scout on her heels, she made her way into the kitchen Thursday morning, certain that she hadn't fared any better in her own bed than Cash did on the vinyl fold-out job at the hospital. Did the kindhearted Texan have to consume her every thought?

She poured herself a cup of coffee, added a splash of hazelnut creamer and leaned against the counter, her gaze drifting to Mr. Jenkins's house. Good thing she had stuff to do in Ouray today. Things that would not only keep her mind off Cash, but also prevent her from considering a trip to Montrose. Things like turning in her loan application and helping Buck with an order, followed by a guided-climbing gig.

She sipped the steaming brew. Yes, busy was good.

"Taryn, honey?" Her mother's voice trailed down the hall. "There you are." She strolled into the room. "Gage just called. He's bringing Emma over. Poor thing has one of those nasty colds, so I said I'd keep her."

Taryn's brother was a good father. Still, being a single dad was tough. And it was times like this when he really needed their help.

"Poor kid." Taryn pouted. "Wish I could stay and play with her, but I have to work."

Scout scratched at the back door.

"Oops. Sorry, baby." Taryn hurried across the room to let her out. "Maybe Scout can keep her company."

"Oh, Emma will love having Scout all to herself."

Taryn peered at her mother over the rim of her mug. "And Scout will enjoy all the attention."

The sun was bright and the temperatures mild as she loaded her gear into her Jeep. A few more days like this and they might actually be rid of some snow. But today, she needed to get to the bank. Though not without another passing glance next door. She couldn't deny her attraction to Cash. If she made a list of qualities of her perfect man, Cash would probably fit every one on the list.

She hopped into the vehicle and fired up the engine. But she was far from anybody's perfect woman.

Shaking off the depressing thought, she cruised down a wet and slushy Main Street. While her fingers kept rhythm with the praise song blaring from her speakers, she wondered how Mr. Jenkins was doing and prayed he'd had a restful night.

She parked in front of the bank, waiting for the tune to end before she hurried inside. "Hi, Patsy."

"Hey, Taryn. What can we do for you today?"

"Is Cam in?"

"Yes, but he's in a meeting."

"Oh." She glanced around the lobby that seemed to be void of customers. Now what should she do?

"Is there something I can help you with?"

She returned her attention to Patsy. "I, well, I don't know. I was just dropping something off."

"You can leave it with me if you like." The woman gathered a stack of papers and tapped them against the top of her desk. "I'll make sure he gets it just as soon as he comes out."

Taryn hadn't envisioned giving the paperwork to anyone else but Cam. She looked at the white envelope in her hand. "I guess that'll be okay." She undid the clasp, licked the glue then reclasped and sealed the envelope. "May I borrow a pen?"

"Sure thing."

Taryn wrote Cam's name in big letters. She wasn't about to risk her paperwork falling into the wrong hands. "Here you go." She passed both the pen and envelope to Patsy.

"All righty, then." Patsy set the envelope on the corner of her desk. "I'll give this to him just as soon as I see him."

Taryn's heart was pounding. "Okay. Great. Thanks, Pats."

Walking to her Jeep, Taryn thought she might pass out. *Lord, please let my application find favor with those deciding.*

No telling how long she'd have to wait. Patience wasn't exactly her virtue. This was one of those times when she was going to have to let go and let God.

When she arrived at All Geared Up a few minutes later, she looked at the front of the building in a whole new light. If things went according to plan, she'd have her own apartment and be a business owner before the high season. Excitement welled inside her. Of course, she didn't own any of the things she'd need for an apartment. Other than her bed. She'd need furniture and kitchen stuff…

She turned off the engine and pocketed her key. Oh, what was she worried about? She hopped out and closed the door. Once her mother found out she was moving, no telling what treasures she'd come up with.

"Good morning, Buck." She whisked past the front counter.

"Morning." He eyed her over his shoulder as she shrugged out of her jacket and hung it in the backroom. "I wasn't expecting to see you today."

Returning to the counter, she pushed up her sleeves. "I'm here to work on that order."

"Order?"

"The one you texted me about yesterday. I told you I'd take care of it this morning."

"Oh, that." He continued to mess with a display of sunscreen beside the cash register. "I thought I texted you back."

"I didn't see anything." She pulled her cell phone out of her back pocket and scrolled through her messages. "Nope."

"Hmph. At any rate, I sent that order off last night."

"You—?"

Removing his reading glasses, he turned to look at her. "I felt bad after you mentioned you were at the hospital, so I played with the computer a bit and eventually got the order to go through." He settled onto his stool. "Sorry you didn't get my message, though. Could have saved yourself the trip." He rubbed the lenses of his glasses with his flannel shirttail. "How is Art anyway?"

She repositioned a couple of sunglasses on a nearby shelf. "I haven't heard anything today. As of late yesterday he was resting as comfortably as could be expected with a broken back."

He held his bifocals up to the light then rubbed some more. "Any idea when he'll come home?"

"Tomorrow, I think, but, like I said, I don't have any updates."

"Well—" he finally settled the glasses back on his nose "—since that order's off your plate, maybe you can run on over to Montrose and see for yourself how he's doing."

That was the last thing she needed to do. "As much as I'd love to see Mr. Jenkins, I'm taking some folks climbing in a little over an hour." She retrieved her jacket.

"Oh. Well, maybe you can go after that."

"Maybe." She reached for the doorknob, feeling a tad annoyed. "Later, Buck."

Two for two. Man, nothing was going as planned today. She glanced at her watch. Of course, that meant she had an hour to play with her favorite four-year-old before meeting her climbing group at eleven.

She hopped into the Jeep as her cell phone jangled in her pocket. "Hello?"

"Taryn, this is Joel. Glad I caught you."

What could her boss at Marmot Mountain Guides want? "Yeah, Joel."

"Hey, that group you were supposed to take today didn't make it."

"What do you mean they didn't make it?" She shoved the key in the ignition, watching icicles drip from the awning of the restaurant next door.

"Their flight was canceled, so they aren't coming in until tonight."

"I see." This day was getting weirder by the minute.

"They'd like to reschedule for tomorrow, if that's all right with you."

Tomorrow. Mr. Jenkins was supposed to come home tomorrow. And since Cash didn't have a car, she'd thought about offering to bring them home. Not that her Jeep would be the most comfortable ride.

"Yeah. Tomorrow will be fine. Same time?"

"Yes."

"Okay. See you tomorrow, Joel." Ending the call, she

set the phone on the seat beside her and started the engine. Looked as though she'd have all day to play with Emma now.

The phone jangled again and Cash's number appeared on the screen. Her pulse quickened. "H-hello?" *For someone you don't want to see, you sure are excited.*

"Good morning." Judging by his voice, he definitely hadn't slept well.

"How's it going?"

"Not too bad. They've already measured Gramps for his brace, and physical therapy is happening any time now."

"Sounds like you've got a busy day." She waved to someone on the walk in front of her Jeep.

"Gramps does, anyway. Hey, I need to ask you a favor."

"Sure."

"Would you have time to pick me up and drive me back to Ouray so I can get my car?"

"Oh. Well, I…"

Have nothing else to do.

But she wasn't planning on spending time with Cash. Her insides twisted with indecision. Then she realized there was only one real choice.

"Of course I will. What time do you want me there?"

Cash hated to leave his grandfather, but with the way the nursing staff doted on the old man, Cash knew he was in good hands. Besides, he wouldn't be gone that long. Just long enough to grab some lunch, a change of clothes and his rental car.

In order to do that, though, he found himself relying on Taryn yet again. But his options were limited. Unlike Dallas, he couldn't just call a taxi.

"I have to admit, I was kind of surprised you answered your phone." He watched her maneuver her Jeep down Highway 550. She'd barely looked at him since they left the hospital. "I thought you said you were taking a group out climbing today."

Both hands on the steering wheel, she stared straight ahead, looking almost stiff. "They postponed." Short and sweet. Just like all the other times she'd addressed him today.

A semi whizzed past them, making the Jeep shudder. Perhaps he shouldn't have called Taryn. He was becoming a nuisance.

"Thanks for coming to get me. Seems I've imposed on you a lot lately."

"You're not imposing, Cash. Besides—" shrugging one shoulder, she sent him a bashful smile "—I owe you."

"Owe me? How?"

Her facial expression changed and she seemed to relax. "I turned in my loan application this morning."

"That's great."

"Yeah. It felt pretty good." Her full-blown smile warmed his heart. "You did an amazing job with the business plan."

"Ah, it was nothing."

"Nothing?" She cast him an incredulous look. "Are you kidding? You saved me. Even if I had managed to pull together a business plan, it wouldn't have looked near as professional as yours. I don't know how I can ever thank you."

"You already did."

Her brow puckered in confusion.

"I don't know what I would have done without your help yesterday. And then agreeing to pick me up today…"

She shrugged again. "What are friends for?"

Friends? He'd be lying if he said he wasn't hoping for more. But he had no intention of giving up.

The pavement hummed beneath the Jeep's heavy-duty tires. Passing through Ridgway, he glanced at the clock on the dash. Was it really almost one o'clock? "Have you had lunch yet?"

"No. I'm not really hungry." Just then her stomach growled, belying her claim.

"Guess somebody forgot to tell your stomach." He grinned at her. "What do you say I buy us some lunch to celebrate your turning in that application?"

"I thought you wanted to get right back to the hospital?"

"A guy's gotta eat sometime." He could tell by the way she chewed her lip that she was debating.

"How about a compromise?"

"I'm listening." And watching. He couldn't seem to take his eyes off her.

"I'll fix lunch for both of us while you gather up your stuff. I'm sure your grandfather has some canned soup and sandwich fixings."

"He does indeed." Though, after what happened the night of Trent and Blakely's wedding, he thought the last thing she'd want was to be alone with him.

"Good." Her wistful expression had him wondering if maybe something had changed between them. If maybe she'd decided to open herself to the possibility of a relationship. Or was that just wishful thinking on his part?

Either way, she'd agreed to have lunch with him. And he'd take any time he could get with Taryn.

His cell phone vibrated in his pocket. He'd kept the thing on silent at the hospital, not wanting to disturb Gramps. Now he pulled it out and looked at the screen. *Dad.* The muscles in his neck knotted.

"Hey, Dad."

"Afternoon, son. Hadn't heard from you today. Thought it best I check in." His father's tone said he knew Cash had decided to stay until Gramps was well. And he wasn't pleased.

"Gramps is resting as comfortably as he can. I guess Mom told you his back is broken."

"She did. How long do you expect you'll be out there?"

"No idea. A week or two, maybe three. Just depends on how Gramps is doing." He stared out the window, watching the open range rush by. Clouds had started rolling in, shadowing what had started out as a beautiful day.

"That's commendable, son, but Home Health can take care of your grandfather. You have a responsibility to Coble Trailers. I'm sure Art will understand."

He'd understand, all right. Understand that Cash had become so all-consumed with work that he didn't have time for family. Not even when it was his fault Gramps fell in the first place.

"The man can't even get out of bed on his own." Raking a hand through his hair, he tried to rein in his emotions. "Look, I'm every bit as committed to the company as I was before I came out here, but I'll have to do some things long-distance for a while."

"What about our customers? Hank Moncrief called looking for you this morning."

"Then I will call Hank back."

"What if he needs you to pay him a visit?" Always the worrier, Dad had a knack for coming up with worst-case scenarios.

"Dad, you act as though business has come to a grinding halt because I'm not there."

"I thought you loved this company."

Cash eyed the red sandstone formations that hemmed them in on the left, certain he'd never said that. Commitment didn't always equal love.

He let go a sigh. "This business has been my top priority for the last ten years." He'd poured blood, sweat and countless sleepless nights into it. "And while I may not be there physically, you can rest assured that our customers will still receive the same attention to detail and customer service that I've always provided."

"Well…I certainly hope so."

Cash wanted to toss his phone out the window. He would never please his father.

Taryn made a left at the Beaumont.

"Where are you now?"

"We're fixin' to pull up to Gramps's house. Taryn brought me back so I could get my car."

"And your computer, I assume?"

He fought the urge to roll his eyes the way he did when he was a teenager. "Of course."

"Good. I need you to send me those latest sales figures."

"I sent them last week."

"Must've gotten lost in cyberspace, then." Or his father had deleted the email without opening the attachment.

"You'll have them in fifteen minutes."

He ended the call, slamming the door as he exited the Jeep.

Taryn fell in line beside him, looking a bit apprehensive.

"I'm sorry you had to hear that."

She shrugged as she continued up the back steps and opened the storm door.

He unlocked the door and followed her into the kitchen. "Should be some soup in the cupboard." He pointed. "Sandwich stuff's in the fridge. I'm gonna boot up my computer."

In the dining room, he waited for his laptop to start. After all these years, did his dad think Cash would forget about the company simply because he wasn't there? He thought he would have proved himself capable by now, but apparently his father would always see him as the loser who thought goofing off with his friends was more important than college.

After connecting to the internet, he pulled up the email he'd sent last week and changed the subject line to read JANUARY SALES before forwarding it to his father. If that didn't get his attention, nothing would.

He checked his in-box and responded to the two emails that needed immediate attention.

"Lunch is ready."

He must have really zoned out, because he almost forgot Taryn was there. He stood and started toward the kitchen. "Smells good."

On the table were two plates, each holding a small bowl of soup, a grilled cheese sandwich that had been cut in half and some potato chips. Beside them, a spoon rested atop a folded napkin.

"Water, milk or something else?" Taryn stood next to the refrigerator.

"Water's good." He pulled out her chair and waited for her to sit down.

"Thank you." Those beautiful eyes peered up at him.

He took the seat across from her. "This looks great."

"It's just soup and a sandwich."

"Yeah, but you made it look special. Like at a restaurant. Thanks."

"You're welcome."

He picked up his sandwich and took a bite.

She watched him then bowed her head for a moment before dipping the spoon into her soup.

She was praying. Why hadn't he thought of that?

Because somehow, in his busy life, he'd gotten away from saying grace.

He massaged the back of his neck.

"You okay?"

"Yeah. Just trying to work out some of this tension."

"You were okay until your dad called." She gave him a pointed look.

He thought back on his day. Despite a rough night on the hard fold-out chair at the hospital, he'd been pretty relaxed all morning. "I guess you're right."

She picked up a chip, broke it in two. "Are you aware that there are two sides to Cash Coble?" She popped one half in her mouth.

"Two sides?"

"Yep. Though I suspect you're not too familiar with one of them."

Wiping his hands with a napkin, he set his elbows on the table. "Do tell, Miss Purcell."

She folded her hands in her lap, refusing to look at him. "One side is relaxed and easygoing. His eyes sparkle with life because he's not afraid to look goofy in front of a bunch of kids or fall prey to the whims of a young woman who kidnaps his laptop, even though he could easily take it back and make a getaway. He makes a little dog who's afraid of everyone adore him in no time at all. And he rushes to rescue those who can't help themselves."

She took a deep breath. "But then there's this other guy. And when he takes over, his whole being morphs. His shoulders become very rigid and his face hardens. He's perpetually rubbing his neck because of the chronic stress that overwhelms him. His heart is good, but he's so busy trying to earn his father's approval, he's forgotten what it's like to live."

She looked at him now, those heart-stopping blue eyes filled with tenderness. "I really wish that first guy was around more often."

Cash swallowed the lump that had formed in his throat. She'd nailed him. Guy number two was his default. What he needed to be to survive. But he liked guy number one a whole lot better. And Taryn seemed to know just how to bring him out. Which was probably why he was so drawn to her.

He cleared his throat, suddenly more concerned with her approval. "Maybe…with a little help, he could be."

Chapter Twelve

Her heart was going to end up broken. Taryn knew that, but it was too late. Whether she wanted to admit it or not, she'd fallen for Cash. A part of her thought, why not ride the tide? Have fun with the sweet Texan who seemed to enjoy her company as much as she did his. But her pragmatic side said the more time she spent with Cash, the harder she'd fall.

Reality was overrated.

Though she spent most of the next day at the ice park, she could hardly wait to get home, change into something much cuter than her climbing gear and rush next door. Now, as darkness settled over the town, she followed Scout up the steps of Mr. Jenkins's front porch, her heart racing.

Cash's rented SUV was in the driveway and lights glowed inside, indicating they'd made it home from the hospital. She couldn't help wondering if his father had called him again. For Cash's sake, she hoped not.

Scout's tail wagged with anticipation as she waited by the door.

"I know exactly how you feel, baby." With a calming breath, Taryn rang the doorbell. She couldn't remember the last time she'd been so eager to see someone.

What about Brian?

She shook the thought away. Cash was not Brian.

The door burst open and Cash stood on the other side of the glass. The smile on his face made her insides flutter. And that had to be the best-looking flannel shirt she'd ever seen. Even though she had seen it before.

Scout wiggled all over when he opened the storm door, half whining, half barking as she bounced at his feet.

"Come here, Scout." He scooped her up. The dog squirmed and licked Cash's face. "Yes, I'm happy to see you, too." His gaze found Taryn's. "Both of you."

Emotions swelled inside her. Giddy, crazy emotions. Emotions she would have dismissed a week ago. Now...?

"How's your grandfather?" She walked past Cash as he held the door. A fire blazed in the fireplace and the evening news was on television. Some things never changed.

"Better now that I'm home, young lady." Mr. Jenkins reclined in his chair, wearing a hard plastic brace around his torso.

Taryn couldn't help smiling as she approached the old man. "Looks like we're going to have to call you Turtle Man." She knelt beside him. "So how are you feeling?"

"I've been better. But I've been worse, too. I'm alive and that means the good Lord ain't done with me yet." He patted her hand.

"Well, I, for one, am very glad to hear that."

Cash had set Scout on the floor and she now bounced alongside the chair.

"No, baby. You can't jump on Mr. Jenkins." She ran a hand over Scout's wiry fur. "You might hurt him."

"Ah, she can't hurt a tough old coot like me." Mr. Jenkins patted his leg, encouraging Scout to join him.

The dog leaped into his lap, then, as though knowing she needed to be careful, settled between his leg and the arm of the chair.

"That's a good girl." Mr. Jenkins stroked the dog's head. Cash touched Taryn's arm. "Come with me."

She followed him to the kitchen.

"You're not gonna believe this." He paused at the Formica-topped table and waited. "I know I sure didn't." He gestured toward the counters.

Plastic containers and foil pans of varying shapes and sizes covered nearly every surface. An outpouring of support from a close-knit community.

"And there's more in here." He opened the refrigerator. Just yesterday the thing had been almost empty. Now it was brimming with pots, casserole dishes and more foil pans. He grinned. "I've never seen so much food."

"Ouray is a small town. Everybody knows everybody. And everyone loves your grandfather." She pointed to an enameled cast-iron pot. "I hope you marked the containers that'll need to be returned."

"They took care of that for me." He closed the fridge door. "But I'll probably need your help figuring out where everybody lives."

"I can do that." She moved to the counter beside the fridge and lifted the aluminum foil from one of the pans. "Mmm. Ida Markum's millionaire pie. Life doesn't get much better than that." She faced Cash. "So, have you eaten?"

"No." He looked confused. "I don't have a clue where to begin."

"That's easy. Just take an inventory of what you've got. Decide what you want to eat tonight and tomorrow, then freeze the rest. That way, nothing will spoil, and all you'll have to do is warm things up in the oven."

"Spoken like someone who knows their way around the kitchen."

"We all have our strengths. You know business plans, I know kitchens. Now—" she shooed him away from the refrigerator and opened the door "—go get a piece of paper and something to write with. You're my list man." Glancing behind her, she noticed he hadn't moved. "What?"

"Will you stay for dinner?"

If she said yes, there would be no turning back.

"Cash, you just don't get it do you? You have Ida Markum's millionaire pie." She gestured to the counter. "Of course I'm staying."

The slow grin that spread across his face said more than any words. He wanted her there. And right now, she couldn't imagine being anyplace else.

Gramps was Cash's number-one priority. Keeping him safe and as comfortable as possible topped Cash's to-do list. Yet for some reason, Gramps couldn't wait to get rid of him.

"I need my mail, son. I've always paid my bills on time and I don't intend to stop now."

Standing beside his grandfather's recliner, he stared down at the old man, wondering why he still kept that old post-office box when home delivery would be so much easier. "But I don't like leaving you alone."

"I'm not alone." Gramps poked a thumb toward the Home Health nurse. "Melissa here plans on giving me quite a workout."

Cash eyed the thirty-something woman.

"That's right," she said. "Today's goal is to teach Art to get out of bed without assistance."

"So while we're working on that, you can pick up my mail. Key's on the hook by the back door." Gramps sure was insistent. Just like Cash's mother.

And whether he wanted them or not, he had his marching orders.

He glanced down at his only pair of jeans and the Henley he'd worn every other day since arriving. "Melissa, how long do you think you'll be here?"

She shrugged. "Hour, maybe longer."

"Excellent." He turned his attention to his grandfather. "I'll be back before you know it."

"Take your time," Gramps hollered behind him.

Cash donned his new jacket before stepping out into the cool afternoon air. He didn't plan on taking any more time than necessary, but there was something he'd like to do besides getting Gramps's mail.

A smattering of clouds played peekaboo with the sun as he walked toward Main Street, contemplating his limited wardrobe. One pair of jeans and four shirts. Enough for three days, but three weeks?

Not quite.

To his surprise, Ouray was bustling this Saturday afternoon. Folks wandered the sidewalks, taking in the sights, and a steady stream of traffic moved up and down Main Street. Here he thought Ouray shut down in the winter. But the ice park seemed to keep things going year-round.

Moving at a relatively brisk pace, he headed toward All Geared Up. From what he'd seen the day he bought his jacket, they had a nice selection of clothing, in addition to everything else. If only Taryn were there to help him. But, as he'd learned last night, she taught children's ski lessons in Telluride on Saturdays. He shook his head with a chuckle. Was there anything she couldn't do?

When he opened the wood-and-glass door at All Geared Up, the store hummed with energy. It wasn't packed but definitely busy. Several people—obvious climbers—huddled around a glass case on an elevated section of the store. Carabiners, ropes and helmets seemed the order of the day.

Cash headed straight for the men's clothing, though with so much stuff in one place, it was difficult to stay focused. He flipped through the hangers on the rack and quickly selected a soft flannel shirt, a long-sleeved T-shirt and another Henley. Now, if he could find a pair of—

Turning, he spotted a short stack of denim jeans, thumbed through the pile until he located his size. All Geared Up seemed to have it all.

Arms loaded, he studied the store once more. Even the rafters held merchandise. Skis, kayaks and one of those toboggans that Taryn had brought to the sledding hill. He could spend hours in here, but not with Gramps waiting on his mail.

Easing toward the checkout counter, he recognized the man at the cash register as Taryn's boss. "You've got quite a place here." He set his items on the counter.

"Why, thank you." The man's gaze narrowed. "Aren't you Art Jenkins's grandson?"

"Yes, I am." He held out his hand. "Cash Coble."

The man took hold. "Buck Ramsey. Good to know you." Letting go, he scanned the bar code on the first shirt. "How's your grandfather?"

"As well as can be expected, I suppose. Pain is still an issue, though if you know my grandfather, you know he'll never complain about it."

Buck nodded in understanding. "We're just thankful he's okay."

"You're not the only one."

"I hear you're going to be staying with him for a while." The owner folded each item.

Word really did travel fast in a small town. "I am. Which is why I need these." He pointed to the clothes. "Figured I'd get something a little more suited to y'all's weather while Home Health is with Gramps."

"Your timing's good, then. They're calling for more snow and some pretty bitter temps, even for us." Buck loaded the items into a bag. "If you have problems with anything, just bring them back with the receipt and we'll get you taken care of."

"I appreciate that." Especially since he didn't take the time to try anything on. Cash handed over his credit card, signed the receipt and took his bag.

He looked around the shop one last time before stepping out into the cold. No wonder Taryn wanted to buy this place. All Geared Up had found their niche. Throw in some advanced marketing and online sales, and he could see this place doubling its sales.

You could do that.

Boy, would he love to.

He continued up the street, in the direction of the post office. All Geared Up was the kind of place he could get excited about. A place he could put his mark on and actually enjoy.

He heaved out a breath. But All Geared Up was Taryn's. And, like it or not, his life was in Dallas.

So, how did he and Taryn ever have a chance of being together?

Taryn knew something wasn't right almost from the moment she and Scout arrived at Mr. Jenkins's house. Last night, Cash had insisted she join them for dinner again this evening. But he didn't appear anywhere near as happy to see her. Matter of fact, he'd barely spoken since she got there and she'd noticed him rubbing the back of his neck more than once.

"Did you talk to your dad today?" She pulled a chicken-and-rice casserole out of the oven and set it on top of the stove.

Cash grabbed plates from the cupboard. "No."

"So what's wrong?"

"What makes you think something's wrong?" He set the plates on the table with a little too much force.

"You're rubbing your neck."

"So. Can't a guy rub his neck without getting the third degree?" His gaze bore into her. "This is me, Taryn. Take it or leave it."

Yep, something was definitely wrong. Cash had never talked to her like that. And as tempted as she was to take him up on his offer and walk out the door, something compelled her to stay. Did she dare try to find out what was going on? Or simply save his grandfather from spending the evening alone with Mr. Grouchy Pants?

When dinner was ready, Mr. Jenkins insisted they all eat at the table. Last night, they'd set up a TV tray beside his recliner, then joined him in the living room so he wouldn't have to eat alone. But tonight he wanted things back to normal.

The old man scooped a forkful of casserole. "Taryn, I want you to take Cash to church tomorrow."

Taryn nearly choked on the bite she'd just eaten.

"Gramps, you know I can't do that." Cash looked way too serious.

"Yes, you can. I talked with Melissa—" Mr. Jenkins's attention momentarily diverted to Taryn "—that's my Home Health nurse." Then back to Cash. "She's going to stay with me so you can go to church."

Taryn's gaze darted between the two men. It was obvious that Cash wasn't pleased, though why, she wasn't sure. Was it because he didn't want to leave his grandfather, didn't want to go to church or didn't want to go with her?

"It's not fair for you to push me onto Taryn like that." Cash fingered a white paper napkin.

"I don't mind." She smiled at him, trying not to take his comment personally.

His grandfather grinned, looking somewhere between mischievous and overly pleased. "Good, that's settled then." He forked another bite. "So Taryn, how did things go over at Mountain Village today?"

"Great. I had a group of four- and five-year-olds that really kept me on my toes." She stabbed a green bean. "But they were so cute."

"Taryn loves kids." Mr. Jenkins addressed his grandson, sounding vaguely like her mother. "Almost as much as they love her." He sent her a wink.

Cash all but glared at her. "I can see that."

As the meal wore on, Mr. Jenkins's chipper demeanor seemed to wane. His smile had shifted into a grim line. He lowered his fork and leaned against the table.

"You okay, Gramps?" Cash stood and moved to his grandfather. "Do you need some more pain medication?"

"Help me back to my recliner, son." Cash eased the old man out of the hard vinyl chair. "Guess I shouldn't have insisted on sitting at the table just yet. These chairs make my tailbone ache."

Since his tailbone had borne the impact of his fall, it stood to reason that it would bother him. Next time, she'd recommend they put a cushion on his seat.

She glanced at Cash. That is, if there was a next time.

While he helped Mr. Jenkins, Taryn cleared the dishes and filled the old white porcelain sink with soapy water.

"Why don't you use the dishwasher?" Cash looked annoyed.

She shrugged. "It was empty. There aren't that many dishes. I can have these—" she gestured to the three plates, utensils and the foil pan "—washed up in no time." She dropped the silverware into the sink. "How's your grandfather?"

"Better."

"Good." She tossed him a towel. "Here, you can dry." He didn't look happy, but he didn't refuse, either.

"So, what did you do today?"

"Nothing much." He scowled.

Dipping her hands in the sudsy water, she knew she had to do something. She'd never seen Cash quite like this. So discouraged and downtrodden. And yet he hadn't talked to his father.

She rinsed the plates and set them in the other side of the sink, eyeing the sprayer.

Cash grabbed one dish and wiped it, his less-than-cheerful attitude still firmly in place.

Desperate times called for desperate measures. With the water still running, she snagged the sprayer, aimed it at Cash and pulled the trigger.

"Hey!"

"You need to lighten up, cowboy."

He stood there with his mouth hanging open. "Why, you little—" He all but dropped the plate, snatched the sprayer and gave her a dose of her own medicine.

She squealed. The collar of her turtleneck was soaked in no time as the water rolled from her face. But growing up with two brothers had served her well. Instinct kicked in. She grabbed a handful of bubbles and tossed them in Cash's direction.

They landed on his hair, eyebrows and nose.

When he swiped a sleeve across his nose, she tried to wrestle the sprayer away from him, only to be hit again. Laughing, she twisted around to avoid another attack.

He laughed, too, his muscular arms coming around her.

"You kids okay in there?"

With one arm holding her firmly around the waist, Cash used the other to hold the sprayer just out of Taryn's reach. "We're fine, Gramps. Just having a little fun." His hold relaxed and she stepped away to see those dimples she liked so much.

He returned the sprayer to its rightful place then closed the space between them. His gaze skimmed over her before connecting with hers. "Sorry. I guess I got a little carried away."

She couldn't help smiling. "Good. Then my madness was successful."

He lifted a hand to tuck a strand of wet hair behind her ear then allowed his fingers to gently trail down her cheek.

"Have I ever told you how good you are for me?"

Her mouth went dry. She swallowed hard. Shook her head.

He tilted her chin to look at him. "You have a way of making the bad stuff fade away. Until all I see is the man I want to be." His words washed over her tattered heart like a healing balm. His woodsy cologne enveloped her, making her forget every reason they shouldn't be together.

Her heart pounded. Surely he could hear it. No doubt Mr. Jenkins could hear it. But, for once, she didn't care. Pushing up on her tiptoes, she kissed Cash.

One arm slid around his neck as he pulled her closer. Lip to lip, heart to heart, she let go of her past and everything else that stood between them, and lost herself in the moment.

When they finally parted, Cash rested his forehead against hers. "I'm sorry for being such a jerk earlier."

She couldn't seem to stop grinning. "That's okay. We all have off days. Just don't make a habit of it."

His laugh was a whisper against her skin. "I suppose I should go check on my grandfather."

She forced herself to take a step back, running into the counter. "Yes, you should. I'll join you just as soon as I—"

His cell phone rang. He pulled it out of his pocket and checked the screen. "It's my mother. Hi, Mom." He listened, his expression serious at first, then the corners of his mouth lifted. "Really? Cool. All right, keep me posted." He ended the call. "My sister's in labor."

"That's wonderful." Yet, as happy as she was for Megan, a twinge of envy sparked inside Taryn.

"I need to tell Gramps." Cash started toward the door. "By the way, he mentioned something about dominoes."

"Sounds like fun." An old ache filled her heart as he disappeared around the corner.

She grabbed the towel and dried her face. The night she went into labor, she was scared and alone. But oh, the joy of holding the life that had grown inside her for nine months. A perfect, beautiful baby boy. She smiled remembering the way he smelled, the way his tiny hand gripped her finger.

Blinking away the unbidden tears, she turned back to the dishes. That was the last time she saw her baby. And though she knew she'd done the right thing by giving him up for adoption, sometimes the incredible pain of saying goodbye crept up on her.

But no one ever knew. And until recently, she never thought anybody except Blakely would know. The way Cash looked at her, though…she wanted to tell him everything about Brian and the baby. To find comfort in his embrace. To hear him whisper that her past didn't matter. That he loved her anyway.

She dipped her hands in the now-lukewarm water. But what if he didn't respond that way? What if he rejected her?

She couldn't go through that again.

Chapter Thirteen

Cash was ready to leave as soon as the Home Health worker arrived. He'd like to say it was because he was eager to get to church. Instead, it had more to do with who would be accompanying him.

He still couldn't believe Taryn had kissed him. He hadn't initiated it, even though he may have wanted to. No, this time it was all her idea.

His mind reeled at the memory. In a matter of seconds, she had completely flipped his mood with her honesty and playful tendencies. No one had ever had that kind of effect on him. But as he kept being reminded, she wasn't just anyone.

Now, as he bounded down the front steps of Gramps's house, she waited beside her Jeep.

The morning sun shone down, glistening off a fresh dusting of snow as he hurried to greet her.

"Ready?" Her smile was beyond contagious.

White puffs billowed behind the vehicle.

"I was born ready." After opening the car door for Taryn, he took a seat on the passenger side. "So, how are you this morning?"

She shifted the Jeep into gear and started down the

street. "Good. Although I think I was playing Chicken Foot in my sleep all night long."

He laughed. "Gramps will get a kick out of that. So, does that mean we can count on you for another game of dominoes in the near future?"

She sent him a sideways glance. "Maybe." Her grip tightened on the wheel. "Any baby news?"

"Yep, there was a text waiting for me when I woke up. I have two new nephews—Noah and Joshua. Everyone is happy and healthy, so hopefully they'll be coming home soon."

"Ah, named after two men who chose to follow God, despite what their peers said."

"I hadn't thought about it, but you're right. That's pretty cool. My dad named me after his favorite singer."

"And who was that?"

He sent her a surprised look. "Johnny Cash, of course."

She grinned. "Well, I'm glad they went with Cash then, because you definitely don't look like a Johnny."

When they arrived at Restoration Fellowship, Cash exited the vehicle and hurried around to help Taryn out.

"Thank you." Her eyes shimmered like the aquamarine stone in one of his mother's rings.

"My pleasure." He offered his elbow and escorted her up the freshly shoveled walk and inside the brick building.

A dozen or so people mingled in the wood-paneled foyer. It was a far cry from his megachurch back home. He may have been away from church for a while, but this was going to be quite a change.

Where two or more are gathered in My name…

The words played across his heart as though God was reminding him not to judge. But not to worry. If God had a word for him today, Cash was ready to hear it.

Laying a hand against the small of Taryn's back, he urged her across the green carpet.

"Taryn!"

She whirled around, squealing when she saw Blakely walking up behind them with her husband. "When did you get back?"

The two friends embraced.

"Last night."

Trent continued toward Cash, grinning. "They're like a couple of schoolgirls."

"Yeah, they are." He shook Trent's hand. "How was the honeymoon?"

"Great. We couldn't have asked for better weather."

"Cash?" Blakely jerked her head in his direction. "You're still here?" Her curious gaze darted between him and Taryn.

He nodded. "Long story, but yes."

"Gran told us about your grandfather." Blakely tucked a strawberry-blond curl behind her ear. "How is he?"

"He's coming along. Still dealing with some pain, but he's in good spirits."

"Now, that's what I like to hear," said Trent. "Because those good spirits will go a long way toward helping him recover."

Blakely looked up at Cash, her concern evident in her puckered brow. "Would it be all right if we paid him a visit?"

"By all means." He stepped out of the way of a mother and father struggling to keep up with two toddlers. "Gramps would be glad to see you."

Blakely smiled. "Good. Maybe we can come by this afternoon?" She glanced up at her husband.

"Works for me."

Piano music drifted from the sanctuary.

"Where's Austin?" Taryn scanned the crowded foyer.

Trent followed Taryn's gaze. "He came early for Sunday school, but he should be out any— Ah, there he is." He tugged Blakely's arm. "We'd better intercept him."

"Talk to you guys later." Blakely waved as they pressed deeper into the foyer.

Taryn looked at Cash. "Guess we better grab a seat, too."

"Lead the way."

They moved through the double doors, the music and chatter growing louder, and slid into the wooden pew alongside Taryn's parents, Phil and Bonnie.

Phil leaned across his wife and Taryn to shake Cash's hand.

"Good morning, Cash." Bonnie beamed.

"Mornin'." Removing his coat, he spotted Dan Carthage, the pastor, coming up the aisle. Not only had he stopped by the hospital, he and his wife had been the first ones to show up with food when Cash and Gramps came home from the hospital Friday.

"Hey, Cash." The brown-haired man rested a hand on his shoulder. "Good to see you again." He nodded to Taryn and her folks before returning his attention to Cash. "Glad you could join us."

"It's good to be here."

"How's Art coming along?"

The pianist transitioned from a contemporary praise song to an old hymn.

"A little bit better every day."

"Guess that's all we can ask for." Dan smiled. "And like I said Friday, don't hesitate to call on us if you need anything."

"I appreciate that. Thank you."

After a quick handshake, the man moved across the aisle to greet someone else.

Taryn leaned toward Cash. "Friday?"

"He and his wife brought food."

"Ah."

After a few more minutes, the pastor took the stage, guitar in hand, and led the thirty or so parishioners in praise-and-worship music. No choir, no special worship leader. Yet, as Cash sang songs he'd sung countless times before, he felt more connected to God than he ever had at his big church in Dallas. There was nothing showy. Just people raising their voices to their Creator.

He'd never felt more at home.

"Do you care more about what people think, or what God thinks?" The pastor began his sermon a short time later. "You know, sometimes doing what is pleasing to God can cost us. It can cost our pride. We might look foolish or unpopular. It can cost us time. And sometimes, doing what God wants can be plain hard."

He paced the altar. "I was on my way to becoming an architect when, shortly after I graduated college, God moved me toward ministry." He paused. "My dad wasn't real thrilled with my decision. Over and over again I heard how he'd wasted money on my education, how I'd never make a good living. And I thought, 'God, is this what You really want from me?'

"You see, I wanted God's approval, but in order to do that, I'd have to sacrifice my father's approval."

Cash straightened. Pastor Dan could have been talking about his life. His dad had never been on board with his plans to live in Ouray or be a civil engineer. Said it wouldn't afford him the kind of life Cash's father had worked so hard to give him. What Dad didn't realize was that Cash didn't want that kind of life. He loved the outdoors. He wanted to be free to enjoy nature. Not stuck behind some desk.

Cash stared at the stained-glass windows, the pastor's voice fading into the background.

No son of mine is going to be a screwup. Cash could

still see the disappointment in his father's eyes as Cash lay in that hospital bed, his leg in a brace. Later, his dad was ready to pull whatever strings it took to keep a failing Cash in school, on one condition. Cash had to switch his major to business.

His father had gotten sick right after Cash graduated. If he hadn't had that business degree, the company might not have survived. So he made the right choice, didn't he?

The pastor continued. "Paul told the Galatians in chapter one, verse ten, 'If I were still trying to please people, I would not be a servant of Christ.' My suggestion to you is choose you this day who *you* will serve. Let us pray."

God, what are You trying to tell me?

Single-digit temperatures did little to deter Taryn from ice climbing. Especially when Blakely agreed to join her. Her friend had been back in town for almost a week and this was their first opportunity to get together. Throw in the fact that Taryn had one of her best climbs on one of Ouray Ice Park's toughest routes, and this was one stellar day.

"Your turn, Blakes." Returning to the bottom of the natural gorge, she untied her knot and retrieved the belay device from her harness.

"Not on your life." Bundled in her heavy coat, Blakely shook her head. "I'm the amateur, remember?"

Taryn was sweating from her climb. "I would hardly call you an amateur, but if you want to be a wienie."

"Throw me in a bun and squirt ketchup and mustard on me then, because I am not trying that route."

"Still not ready to try mixed climbing, huh?" She eyed the ice- and water-polished rock above them. "Fine. We can call it a day." Taryn unhooked her length of rope and started to reel it in while Blakely packed her gear.

"Now, let me see if I've got this straight." Her friend

stood and slung her pack over her shoulder. "Cash rescued a family who drove off the road, so he couldn't make his flight when they closed the pass. Then his grandfather fell, breaking his back, so Cash is staying to take care of him."

Talking while climbing had been a challenge since they almost had to yell, but then everyone else in the park might hear them, so their conversation had been limited. Sounded like Blakely had caught the high points, though.

"That about sums it up." As her body temperature adjusted, Taryn donned her coat.

"Man, I should leave town more often." Blakely toed at a chunk of snow-covered ice. "And you've spent every evening with him?"

"I've been helping him and his grandfather with meals and stuff. Oh, and there's something I haven't told you."

Blakely picked up the coil of rope. "What? You're engaged?"

"Very funny." Taryn hoisted her pack, grabbed the rope from her friend and started for the walk up. "Now you'll have to wait until we get up top."

Her friend groaned as she turned to follow. "You're such a brat sometimes."

"Yeah, but you love me anyway." And that was true. Blakely knew everything about her. The good and the bad, and she loved her anyway. If only she could count on others to love her like that.

"I'm buying All Geared Up," she said once they were topside and across the bridge. "Well, nothing's for sure yet, but I turned in my loan application last week. Cash knew everything about business plans, so he put together an amazing package for me."

Her friend grabbed her elbow, stopping her. "Wait a minute. Why are you buying All Geared Up? You're the best mountain guide in town. Why would you give that up?"

Taryn's excitement dissipated. "Not you, too."

"What do you mean?"

"The few people I've told have all said similar things. So I have to give up being a guide. It's not like I have to give up climbing." She started walking again. "I thought you, at least, would be on my side."

Blakely jogged to catch up, her breath white puffs in the frigid air. "I am on your side. I guess I'm just a little surprised, that's all. What made you decide to do this?"

Taryn opened the back door of her Jeep and tossed in her gear. "Because I need something that's mine. I'm twenty-seven years old and I still live with my parents."

Blakely tossed her pack in, too. "I'm about to turn thirty and I just left my grandparents, so don't try that with me."

"Yeah, but that's different. You have Austin." Closing the door, she leaned against the Jeep and watched the vehicles coming off the mountain, winding their way down the Million Dollar Highway. "I have no one. So I need to build a life for myself. A future. Besides, who knows more about what gear climbers need than I do?"

"Well, I'll give you that one." Blakely shivered. "Can we get in the car? It's cold out here."

They got into the Jeep, and Taryn started the engine, waiting for the heater to kick in as Blakely pulled a thermos from the floorboard.

"Hot chocolate?"

For the moment, it was colder inside the Jeep than out. "I thought you'd never ask."

Blakely filled a cup and handed it to Taryn. "Have you thought this all the way through? Running a business is tough. You remember all the struggles I had last summer. I had no idea the amount of stuff Granddad had on his plate."

Taryn held the cardboard cup with both hands, allowing the warmth to thaw her now-frozen fingers. "I already do most of the ordering and stocking."

"Okay, but what about managing? Hiring, firing and scheduling employees? Payroll?"

"I'm sure I can learn."

Her friend took a sip and stared out the window. "I'm sure you can, too. You're relatively smart."

"Hey, what do you mean 'relatively'?"

Blakely broke into a grin. "Gotcha." She took another sip. "Seriously, if this is what you're passionate about, I think you could do a fabulous job."

"Thanks."

"Now, about Cash." Blakely twisted to face her.

"What about him?"

"What's going on between you two?"

"Nothing. We're just friends."

"I doubt that."

She sure wished that heat would kick in. "What do you mean?"

"Cash is totally into you, Taryn."

"No, he's—"

"And, dare I say, you're pretty into him, too."

Taryn's default was to reject the notion. But Blakely knew her too well. And right now, Taryn could use a friend to help her sort out her conflicting emotions.

"Well, I can't speak for Cash, but yeah, I really like him." There—it was out. She'd finally admitted—out loud—how she felt.

"Sweetie, you don't need to speak for Cash. It's written all over his face whenever he looks at you."

"But he doesn't *know* me."

"You mean, your history?"

She nodded, the steam from her drink warming her face.

"He seems like a decent guy. I'm sure he'll understand."

The blower finally kicked on.

"Understand that I let myself fall for someone who was

just using me?" She shook her head. "I'm such an idiot. Why would someone like Cash even bother with me?"

Blakely's gaze narrowed, her lips pursed. "Taryn Purcell, you stop that right now. I don't know what kind of lies Brian filled your head with, but you are not an idiot. Yes, you were young and naive, but you've grown into an incredible woman. Any man who doesn't see that isn't worthy of you anyway."

Something between a sob and laughter bubbled out of her. "Okay, *Mom.*"

Laughing, Blakely swatted her leg. "When you stop acting like a child, I'll stop acting like your mother."

"Unfortunately, I don't think my mother would be quite so understanding."

Growing serious, her friend took hold of her hand. "You say that, but I've never felt like your mother looked down on me for having Austin. Maybe she's mellowed."

"Maybe. But then, you're not her daughter." She turned slightly to face her friend. "I just remember when I was about nine, the Barkers' daughter got pregnant. Mom and I were in one of the stores and overheard people talking about it. Mom was furious. When we left, she grabbed hold of my arm and said, 'Let's get one thing straight right now, young lady. No daughter of mine will ever have a child out of wedlock. I will not have people talking about my family. If you ever do that to me, I'll disown you.'"

Blakely's grip tightened. "Taryn, we've all made mistakes. I mean, just look at me and Trent." She continued to watch her. "You know, I remember a certain someone chastising me for not letting go and letting God. Sounds like you need to do a little letting go yourself."

Taryn took a deep breath and pulled her hand free to swipe at a wayward tear. "I don't know why we're having this conversation anyway. Cash will be going back to Dallas soon. And, if everything goes according to plan,

I'll be settling in at All Geared Up." She downed the rest of her hot chocolate. "Doesn't mean I can't enjoy his company right now." Because she really did like spending time with him. Liked the way he made her feel. As though she really was special.

"No, it doesn't." Her friend smiled. "I just don't want you selling yourself short and closing the door to anything God might have planned for you. Because while you may not believe it, you deserve to be loved."

Chapter Fourteen

Over the past week, Cash had carved out a nice little routine. Up early, he'd fix breakfast for himself and Gramps before settling into his makeshift office. He had his laptop and his phone, and since his assistant mailed him the paperwork he'd left on his desk at Coble Trailers, he was caught up. Possibly for the first time ever.

Of course, he didn't have his father barging into his office at least five times a day, either. Maybe he should have considered working from home a long time ago.

Then there were the evenings spent with Taryn. They were undeniably his favorite part of the day. She'd had dinner with them every night since Gramps got home, usually preparing the meal, whether heating up something others had brought or whipping up her own dish. Cash liked helping her in the kitchen. Liked seeing her at the end of the day. Liked everything about her.

Gramps was improving faster than Cash expected, though. Which meant Cash would be leaving sooner rather than later. But, for now, the old man still needed him, and Cash wasn't about to let him down.

While his grandfather settled in for his afternoon nap in his recliner, Cash made himself comfortable on the couch and enjoyed the fire. One of many things he'd miss about Ouray.

Phone in hand, he pulled up the Bible app he'd downloaded forever ago but hadn't used nearly enough. He'd gone to church again yesterday. This week the pastor focused on the verse from the book of Matthew that talked about seeking God first and then allowing Him to take care of all the other stuff. Cash had heard that verse all his life, even singing a song about it when he was a kid. Though he'd never really grasped what it said until Pastor Dan talked about it.

One thing was for sure. The amount of seeking Cash had done in the last fifteen years would fit into a thimble. Yeah, he was always asking God for stuff, but to genuinely seek Him and entrust every aspect of life to Him? It had been a long time.

Something he needed to change. Starting now.

His phone vibrated in his hand and his dad's name appeared on the screen. Good thing he'd made a habit of turning off the ringer whenever Gramps was asleep. Standing, he moved from the living room through the kitchen and into the laundry room, closing the door behind him.

"Hello."

"Did you get that quote off to Jurikson Motors?"

Less than an hour after it came in. Man, the older his father got, the more crass he became.

"Hello, Cash. How's it going? Oh, pretty good. How 'bout yourself, Dad?" He closed the lid on the washing machine.

"Sorry. Guess I did sorta fly off the handle there."

"Sorta?"

"Yeah, well…" His father grumbled.

Cash leaned against the dryer. "To answer your question, though, yes. It was sent before ten-thirty their time. Why? Didn't they get it?"

"I don't know. I got some message to call them regarding a quote, so I just wanted to make sure." The man really needed to lighten up.

Hmm…sounded like Cash was channeling Taryn.

He grinned. "Did you go see the babies this weekend?"

"Sure did." Was that a smile he heard in his father's voice? "Cute little fellas. Patrick's just about bustin' at the seams with pride over them two."

Sounded to Cash like Patrick wasn't the only one.

"That reminds me, Patrick's folks are due in today, so it looks like your mother should be able to take your place in a couple of days."

"A couple—?" Cash nearly choked on the words. The muscles in his neck knotted. He wasn't ready to leave. Things were going so well here. *He* was doing so well.

"I'll let her give you all the details on her arrival. It sure will be good to have you back here, son."

Good for whom? Certainly not Cash.

He rubbed the back of his neck. "Okay, Dad. I need to go. I'll talk to you later." Returning to the kitchen, he dropped into one of the vinyl chairs. *God, why are You sending me back now?*

He glanced at his phone. When the call ended, it had gone back to the app he'd opened before. Matthew 6:33 stared up at him.

But seek first the kingdom of God and His righteousness, and all these things shall be added to you.

"Okay, God. You win." Cash had been doing things his way for far too long. Maybe if he did things God's way, he wouldn't be so miserable. Besides, God had thwarted his plans to leave twice before. Now Cash could only pray He'd do it again.

More than a week had passed since Taryn turned in her loan application and she had yet to hear anything. To say she was getting antsy would be an understatement. So when she left All Geared Up at four o'clock on Monday afternoon, she hopped into her Jeep and headed straight for the bank, praying Cam was still in.

The sun had dipped below Twin Peaks, bathing the town in shadows. A chill ran through her as she parked and hurried up the bank steps.

"You looking for Cam?" Patsy eyed her as soon as she walked into the lobby.

"As a matter of fact, I am. Is he in?"

Patsy pointed toward his office. "Sure is. You can go on in."

Taryn's palms grew sweaty as she approached the stuffy room. Cam was hunched over his desk, reading glasses perched on the end of his nose, as he stared at his computer. Her pulse raced. She rapped on the door with her knuckles.

His bald head popped up. "Taryn. I was just about to call you. Come on in."

As she sat on the edge of the chair opposite his desk, he moved to close the door. "Little nippy out there today, isn't it?"

She peeled off her headband. "Better than last week." At least now they were into double-digit temperatures.

Returning to his ever-creaking chair, he pulled out a file and scrubbed a hand over his face. "I hate to tell you this, Taryn, but your application has been denied."

Her nervous smile flattened into a thin line. Her heart plummeted as her future evaporated right before her eyes. "Are…are you sure? That was an excellent package I gave you."

"Yes, it was very well put together." He removed his glasses. "However, you just don't have enough capital to support such an undertaking."

"Capital? So I have to have more money?"

"Or assets. You might consider a cosigner. Something that would garner you more financial backing."

Her mind reeled, Cam's words fading into the background. "I see." She swallowed hard, feeling as though her world had been ripped apart. What was she supposed to do now? Standing, she reached for the doorknob.

"I'll hang on to your application, Taryn. Just let me know what you'd like to do."

What she'd like is to get out of here. Fast. She moved through the lobby as quickly as she could, though it still felt like slow motion. Was everyone looking at her? Did they all know that she'd been rejected?

Cold air slammed into her face as she blew through the lobby door, stinging her eyes. Tears formed. She would not cry. She would not—

A single tear spilled onto her cheek. She quickly swiped it away with a gloved finger. Pulling her headband back on, she trudged up the street. Where had she parked anyway?

She stopped. Did an about-face and strode back in the direction of the bank and sought refuge inside her Jeep. She shoved the key in the ignition and fired up the engine.

She slammed the vehicle into gear and started up Main Street. *God, I thought this was what I was supposed to do. What You had called me to.* She'd prayed long and hard before making the decision to move forward on this. Okay, maybe not so long, but definitely hard.

But did you wait for God to answer?

"Yes. No." She let go a sigh. "Maybe." She turned up Fifth Avenue. Why else would God have brought Cash into her life right when she was in need of a business plan?

She pulled up in front of her parents' house. *Lord, I'm floundering here. You know the desires of my heart. I have to start building my own life. Show me what You want me to do.*

Her head ached. She got out of the vehicle, eyeing the light in the window next door. She really wanted to see Cash. Maybe he could help her make sense of things.

She quickly retrieved Scout, hugging her against her chest, and went next door.

The sky was turning dark when Cash's happy face greeted her. Though his smile quickly faded. "Uh-oh. What's wrong?"

That was all it took. Nuzzling her nose into the fur on Scout's neck, she lost it. The floodgates opened and Taryn was a teary, snotty mess.

She turned away, but he caught her by the arm. "No. Don't look at me."

Ignoring her, he pulled her into his arms and held her close.

Scout protested, so Cash took the fidgety pup and set her inside the house.

"You should go in too," Taryn said as he held her once again. "It's freezing out here."

"I don't know. You feel pretty warm to me." He rested his chin atop her head, his hands moving up and down her back. "So, are you going to tell me what's wrong?"

With a giant, very unfeminine sniff, she pulled free and dug out a tissue from her pocket. She blew her nose, another not-so-ladylike move, and regained her composure.

He watched her, arms folded across his chest. "Better?"

She nodded and tucked the tissue back where it came from.

"Would you prefer to continue this conversation out here or go in the house?"

"We can go in."

After ditching her coat and greeting Mr. Jenkins, Taryn followed Cash into the kitchen. Seemed they spent most of their time there lately.

He pulled out a chair for her, scraping it across the worn sheet vinyl. "Can I get you something to drink?"

"No. I'm just being a ninny."

"Well—" he eased into the chair beside her, his grin making her want to throw herself back into his arms "—you're the cutest ninny I've ever seen."

"Hardly." She wiped both hands across her face. "I probably look a mess."

"Never." He took hold of her hands. "Now, what's going on?"

"The bank turned down my loan." She was definitely making progress. She got the words out without a single sob, whine or tear.

"Aw, Taryn…I'm sorry." His thumbs caressed her knuckles. "Did they say why?"

"I don't have enough collateral. Or did he say capital?"

"Doesn't matter. I understand what they're getting at."

"I don't know what I'm going to do, Cash. I wanted this so bad." Her head dropped.

"Why?"

"Why what?"

He tucked a finger under her chin and tilted it until she looked at him. "Why do you want All Geared Up?"

"Because I want something that belongs to me. I mean…I still live at home, I work three different jobs—"

"As do a lot of people in Ouray."

"I suppose." She grabbed a paper napkin off the table and twisted it in her fingers. "But I need a life. And I really like All Geared Up. I don't want to see someone buy it and turn it into another gift shop. It's important to me."

Cash cocked his head, his gaze never leaving her. "Did the loan officer mention anything about a cosigner?"

"Yes."

"Well, what about your folks? Do you think they'd be willing?"

"I don't know." She looked into his green eyes so warm and caring. "At this point, they aren't even aware I want to buy All Geared Up. Let alone that I went to the bank."

"How come you never told them?"

She shrugged. "I was afraid they'd try to talk me out of it." Despite a relatively good relationship, she wasn't exactly in the habit of sharing the important things in her life with her parents.

"Remember in church last week when Pastor Dan talked about God's approval versus man's approval?"

"Yeah." She tore the napkin into tiny strips.

"Sometimes we have to exercise a little bit of faith. If God wants you to have All Geared Up, He'll make it happen, Taryn. But I really think you should talk to your parents."

Probably not a bad idea. "I'll think about it." She stood and crossed to the trash bin. She deposited the sacrificial napkin.

Scout trotted into the kitchen and bounced at Taryn's feet.

"What are you doing, baby?" She picked up the dog and gave her a squeeze. "Has Mr. Jenkins been feeding you treats?"

Scout licked her cheek.

"Speaking of eating…" Cash stood. "I hope you'll grace us with your company again."

"Hmm…what's on the menu?" Something did smell yummy.

He moved past her. "Believe it or not, I already have dinner squared away."

"Really?" She nuzzled Scout with her cheek. She'd been in charge of their meals most nights, a role she'd grown quite fond of, taking care of these two magnificent men.

"Lasagna is already in the oven." He flipped on the oven light to prove his point.

"Nice."

"I put it in right before you rang the bell." He gestured to the counter then. "And to go with it, I've got salad and garlic bread."

She couldn't help smiling. "Well, aren't you the picture of domesticity."

"That would be a big negative." He inched closer and rubbed Scout's head. "But will you please stay anyway?"

She looked up at him, knowing she was going to be an absolute mess when he went back to Dallas. "Sure. Why not."

Cash crawled into the old iron bed after another enjoyable evening. This past week had been a far cry from his nights in Dallas. Those were usually spent at the office, eating some sort of takeout while he continued to work until he could hardly keep his eyes open.

He was glad he'd been able to cheer Taryn up. He didn't like to see her so upset. And it took all the restraint he had not to offer to help her financially. He could do that in a heartbeat. And a week ago, he probably would have. Now he knew he needed to talk to God first and find out what He wanted before offering anything.

He closed his eyes. *So what do You say, God? You already know the situation. Is Taryn buying All Geared Up part of Your plan? If it's not, please reveal that to her and give her peace. But if it is, am I supposed to have a part in it? Should I offer to help her?* Maybe he could be a silent partner. At least that would give him a reason to come back to Ouray more often.

His eyes opened and he stared into the blackness. *I'm falling in love with her, Lord. Could it be that You want her in Dallas? With me?*

Now he was putting thoughts into God's head. He rolled over and fluffed his pillow. He never would have guessed he could change so much in just a few short weeks. *I don't want to go back to the man I was. Help me, Lord.*

What he wouldn't give to live in Ouray. To have the kind of life he used to dream of, back when he used to dream. *Are You there, God?*

Stupid. He knew God was there, listening.

Maybe that's what he needed to do. Shut up and listen.

I'm here, God, whenever You're ready to lay something on me. Today, tomorrow...I'll be listening.

Chapter Fifteen

Taryn made sure she was up and ready to join her parents for breakfast Tuesday morning. She'd fallen asleep last night praying the Lord would give her the right words to say when she approached them about cosigning. But her nerves were still getting the best of her. Which was kind of weird since, overall, she had a good relationship with her parents. Still, she did have a tendency to hold back whenever she thought they might not approve.

"Hey, princess." Her dad was sitting at the table when she walked into the kitchen. His silver hair had that still-wet sheen. "Isn't it kind of early for you?"

"No." She kissed his freshly shaven cheek. "Just for Scout. She's still crashed in my bed." She continued to the coffeemaker, poured a cup and added some hazelnut creamer before joining her father at the table.

"Care for some oatmeal, honey?" Her mom was still in her robe, heating up breakfast for herself and Dad. Their cholesterol level must be outstanding.

"No, thanks." Cradling the warm cup in her hands, she took a sip of the steaming brew. "I would like to talk to you guys about something, though."

Her father folded the newspaper he'd been reading and set it on the table. "What's up?"

Her mom joined them, carrying two bowls. She set one in front of Dad, then took her seat next to him. "Okay, I'm all ears."

Here goes nothing. "I want to buy All Geared Up."

Her parents looked at each other. That silent exchange between parents that's like a language only they understand.

Her dad stirred a spoonful of sugar into his oatmeal. "When did you decide this?" His voice was firm yet calm. Making her even more nervous.

"A few weeks ago." She ran a finger around the rim of her mug. "I've already turned in my loan application to Cam."

Her mom started to take a bite then stopped. "Without telling us?"

"I'm sorry, Mom." She shrugged. "But I was afraid that you might try to talk me out of it. This was something I needed to do on my own."

"So why do you suddenly want to buy a business?" Her dad scooped his first bite.

"All Geared Up isn't just any business. It fits me. I mean, who knows more about what the outdoor enthusiast likes than an outdoor enthusiast?" She lifted her cup. "Besides, I'm thinking about my future. You and Mom don't want me living with you forever. I'll be able to live in one of the apartments over the store."

"And the other one?" her father asked.

"Rent it out. See? Automatic income." She took a drink.

"But we love having you with us." Her mother pouted.

"Mom, it's okay. I'll only be around the corner. Besides, I'll need you to help me decorate and furnish it."

That made her mother smile.

"Has your loan been approved?" Her dad's blue eyes met hers.

"Not exactly." She set her mug on the table. "Seems I don't have enough collateral. Which is why I wanted to talk to you." She took a deep breath. "Would you guys be willing to cosign for me?"

Her dad looked at her mom and vice versa.

He left his spoon in the bowl and leaned back in his chair. "Owning a business is a huge commitment. You've seen how many people have set up shop over the years, only to be gone after one season."

"And what about your climbing?" There was that question again. Except her mother punctuated it with another pout.

"I'll still climb. I just won't guide anymore."

"But you love being a guide."

"I know, but I can't do it forever."

She addressed her father. "All Geared Up is a thriving business with a proven record. I don't plan to do anything that would jeopardize that."

Leaning forward, her dad rested his elbows on the oak table. "Your mother and I will need to pray about this and take a look at our finances." He looked straight at Taryn. "I assume you've prayerfully committed this to the Lord?"

"I've been praying, yes." Though she couldn't exactly say that she'd committed it. More like grabbed the ball and ran with it. Still, she felt God had a hand in this.

"All right, then." Her dad picked up his spoon again and sent Taryn a wink. "I guess we'll just see what the Lord has to say."

"Thank you, Dad." She should have known they'd be willing to at least consider cosigning for her. And talking to them wasn't nearly as bad as she'd feared. Actually, she was glad she'd discussed this with them.

Maybe there are some other things you should discuss with them.

She shook her head. Her past was another matter altogether.

The sound of tiny paws bounding down the stairs caught her attention.

"Sounds like somebody's finally awake." She twisted in her chair to see her baby running toward her, smiling. Yes, Scout was definitely smiling.

The dog pranced from person to person, wiggling and waggling on her way to the back door.

Her mom and dad both greeted her with a pat.

"Ready to go outside?" Taryn stood, cup in hand, and moved to the door. Cold air sifted into the room when she opened it.

"You climbing today?" Her mother glanced her way.

Taryn headed for the coffeepot for a refill. "Hopefully. Joel wanted me to come in and help him inspect some of the gear."

But you love being a guide.

Her mother's comment played through her mind as she stirred creamer into her drink. Why were so many people questioning her decision to give up guiding?

Leaning against the counter, she took a sip. She really did love being a guide. Teaching people to overcome their fears, encouraging them to break out of their comfort zone and push themselves harder. Sometimes it was almost like a therapy session, teaching families and friends to trust each other and work together.

Yeah, she'd miss that.

Climbing meant a lot to her. Had helped her heal. Empowered her to press on and understand that life is a journey not a destination. And she was passionate about sharing that with others.

Could she really give that up?

If she bought All Geared Up, she'd have to.

She shoved away from the counter. Or maybe not.

What if All Geared Up offered climbing clinics? Rock climbing in the summer, ice climbing in the winter. Kind of an introduction to climbing. And if she marketed them just right, she could pull in people who might not have ever considered climbing.

Excitement bubbled inside her. This could actually work.

A bluesy piano riff echoed from Cash's phone Wednesday morning. Sitting at his desk, he hit Send on his first email of the day before answering. His mother's call could only mean one thing.

She was on her way.

"Hey, Mom." He leaned back in the wooden captain's chair.

"Hi, honey. I'm at my gate and my flight is on time, so I should be at the house about two this afternoon."

Cash fingered a small stack of papers. He knew his mother was eager to see firsthand how Gramps was doing, but he still couldn't help wishing she'd held off another day or two. "Do you need me to pick you up at the airport?"

"No, you stay with your grandfather. I'll grab a rental. I'll want my own car once you're gone anyway."

Gone. It sounded so final.

"Okay. Well—" he rubbed the back of his neck "—I guess we'll see you when you get here then."

Standing, he set his cell back on the table and joined his grandfather in the living room. "That was Mom. She says she'll be here about two."

"Hope she's got lots of pictures of those young'uns." Gramps peered up at him from his recliner.

"I don't think you'll have to worry about that." He

wouldn't be surprised if his mother had filled an entire scrapbook already.

"Guess this means you'll be leaving soon."

Cash dropped into the chair on the other side of the fireplace. "Unless you can come up with a way to keep me here."

Gramps shook his head. "I'm not falling off any more ladders."

They both laughed. Something Cash was glad they were able to do, considering how frightening the ordeal had initially been.

The old man's folded hands lay atop his turtle-shell brace. "Cash, I've seen a remarkable change in you since you've been here."

"Me, too." He'd come a long way in the last three weeks. And he liked the man he'd become. He didn't want to be the workaholic Cash anymore. Yet he feared that was exactly what would happen once he returned to Dallas. "I hate to leave."

"Well, maybe you can get back here a little more often. We're just a plane ride away whenever you need to fill your Ouray tank."

"I know." He rose and grabbed two logs from the bin on the hearth. "And next time, I'm definitely flying into Montrose." Opening the glass doors, he laid the wood atop the dwindling flames. They sparked, a puff of smoke drifting into the room.

"Lot quicker." Gramps's smile didn't reach his eyes. "I'm gonna miss having you around."

Cash closed the doors and returned to his seat. "Why does life have to be so complicated, Gramps?"

"I wish I knew, son." The old man paused as though carefully choosing his words. Odd, since he usually spoke his mind. His brow furrowed. "You're not happy in Dallas, are you, Cash?"

"No, sir. Though I don't think I realized it until after you fell and I really allowed myself to settle in here." He pulled the lever to bring up the footrest. "Things are just different in Ouray. People actually take the time to enjoy life."

Gramps retrieved his coffee cup from the side table. Took a drink. "You were able to work from here these last couple weeks. Maybe you could do that permanently, just fly back to Dallas every now and then."

"You make it sound so easy." He rubbed his thumbs across the velvety fabric on the arms of the chair. "And while I could see it working, Dad would never go for it. You know how many times he's called me."

"Well, then…I guess your only choice is to do what you have to do and let God take care of the rest."

"Yeah, I just wish He'd work a little faster." Suddenly restless, he dropped the footrest, crossed to his work area and picked up his own cup.

"Sounds like somebody needs to pray for patience."

"Already did," he hollered over his shoulder on his way to the kitchen for a refill.

"Where's Taryn today?" Gramps asked when he returned. "She climbing?"

"Yeah." He paused beside the old man. "She should be by tonight."

The old man stared across the room at nothing in particular. "I believe saying goodbye to her is going to be your greatest challenge."

Cash looked out the window to the house next door. Leaving Taryn was going to be the hardest thing he'd ever done. "I really like her, Gramps."

"I know you do. And I'm thinkin' she feels the same way about you."

"Perhaps." He wandered to the other side of the room

and watched out the front window. "But she's said more than once that she'll never set foot in Texas again."

"Maybe she hasn't had the right incentive."

He took a sip, eyeing the snow-covered Amphitheater. "I don't know."

"Back in my day they used to say that absence makes the heart grow fonder. Maybe she'll have a change of heart after you're gone."

He faced his grandfather now. "Can you add that to your prayer list?"

Gramps sent him two thumbs-up. "You got it."

Cash returned to his computer. He still had work to do. Though how much he'd actually accomplish remained to be seen.

"When are you planning to leave?"

He ran a finger over the touch pad. Highlighted an email. "I don't know. I need to check flights, see what's available." He put his cup on the table and sat down. "But I'm not going to rush. Week's half over, so I may as well wait until this weekend."

"Now you're talking." Gramps uprighted his chair and slowly pushed to his feet. "Enjoy a few more days in Ouray." He shuffled toward Cash. "Maybe you can even get Taryn to take you climbing again."

He looked up at the man. "*That* sounds like a plan."

Taryn bounded down the oak staircase of her parents' house. Late getting home from her climbing gig, she grabbed a quick shower and changed clothes. For whatever reason, she was even more excited about spending time with Cash tonight. She'd grown fond of their nightly ritual. Dinner, maybe cards, dominoes or some TV. Stuff other people might think boring. But with Cash, everything was fun.

"Do you have a minute?" Her father stopped her at the bottom step. "Your mother and I would like to talk to you."

"Um…sure. Yeah. Okay." She glanced at her watch. *Five forty-five.* Mr. Jenkins didn't like to eat late.

"It won't take long." Her mother looked nervous.

They gathered in the living room, Taryn perched on the edge of the wing-back chair while her folks sat side by side on the leather sofa.

"What's going on?" She'd rarely seen her parents this somber.

"This…is very hard to say." Her dad cleared his throat, a sure sign he was troubled. "We're not going to be able to cosign the loan for you."

"Oh." She kept a straight face, but inside she was falling to pieces. Her parents were her last hope. Without their help, her dream of owning All Geared Up, no matter how short-lived, was gone. Just like every other dream.

"I was prepared to say yes until I delved deeper into our finances." Her dad shook his head. "We just can't do it right now, Taryn."

She stared at her hands. "I understand." If they couldn't afford it, they couldn't afford it. But the pain was still there.

"Perhaps this is God trying to nudge you in a different direction." Her mom sent her a woeful smile. "Honey, I'm not sure All Geared Up is right for you. I mean, if it's a place of your own you want, why don't you look into buying a house or a condo?"

How was a house going to take care of her in her old age? Provide an income when she could no longer guide? She shook her head. How could she expect her mother to understand? She had Dad to take care of her. Taryn had no one. She'd always be alone. Whatever dreams she had of a husband or family died in Texas.

But they didn't know that.

She looked at the two wounded people across from her. Her parents would do anything to help her. Telling her no was difficult for them. No matter how much she ached, she wouldn't add to their distress.

She stood and crossed to her father. "It's okay, Dad. Really." She hugged him. Maybe, deep down inside, she knew her parents would say no. Not to hurt her, but because they truly weren't able to help.

"I'll figure something out." She released him. "If God wants it to happen, I know it'll happen." She said the words with much more conviction than she felt. *Forgive me, Lord. But I don't want them to feel bad.*

She scooped up Scout, who'd been clinging to her since she got home. She'd gotten used to going next door every night, too.

"Think about what I said." Her mother sent her a pleading look.

"I will." She knew better, but she had to put on a good face. "Now, I really need to get next door."

Her mom sniffed. "Spending the evening with Cash again?" When it came to love, the woman shifted gears faster than any race car driver.

"And his grandfather." She started for the door, suddenly more eager to escape than to see Cash.

Outside, she gulped for air, trying to hold herself together. She did not want Cash to see her crying again. *God, I thought You'd presented this opportunity just for me. Now it seems almost impossible.*

She set Scout on the ground. "You need to take care of business, baby." Scout tiptoed through the snow, looking for just the right spot.

Hands burrowed in her pockets, Taryn glanced at Mr. Jenkins's house. A car she hadn't seen before sat in the driveway. They'd had a lot of visitors lately. Considering her mood, perhaps she should wait.

She shivered.

Or not.

"Come on, Scout. Let's go see Cash." She could keep it together. She had to.

Tail wagging, the dog scampered ahead of her, straight up the front steps.

Taryn knocked on the door.

A split second later it opened.

A woman smiled through the glass. Her blond hair was cut in a layered bob and her green eyes were all too familiar.

She pushed open the storm door. "Taryn. How nice to see you again."

Scout planted all fours firmly on the porch and barked at Cash's mom.

"You must be Scout." The woman knelt and held out her hand. "Aren't you the cutest thing? I've heard a lot about you."

Scout sniffed, wagged her tail then trotted inside, as usual.

Taryn followed. "When did you get here, Elise?"

Cash's mother hugged her. "A few hours ago." She shut the door behind Taryn.

"I was hoping that was you." Cash sauntered down the stairs, his dimples carved deep into each cheek.

Turning, Taryn looked from Cash to his mother and back again. With Elise here, that meant…

Cash was leaving.

The emotions she'd been battling clogged her throat. She swallowed hard. She had to get out of here. And the sooner the better.

Scout zoomed across the room just then and bounced at Cash's feet.

He picked her up. "Nice to know somebody missed me."

He scratched under her chin, his gaze riveted to Taryn, as though wondering if she'd missed him, too.

Elise crossed to her father. Standing behind him, she laid her hands on his shoulders. "I can't thank you enough, Taryn. I understand you've been taking good care of these two gentlemen."

"It was nothing." She shrugged.

"Don't listen to her, Mom." Cash set Scout on the floor and placed his hand in the small of Taryn's back, urging her farther into the room. "We would have been lost without her."

"That's for sure." Mr. Jenkins welcomed Scout into his lap. "You've been good medicine for both of us, Taryn."

"Dinner's almost ready." Elise smiled. "Please say you'll join us."

"Oh, well, I…I should be going. I'm sure you all have lots of catching up to do." She started to turn, but Cash grabbed hold of her hand. When she looked up at him, confusion and disappointment marred his features.

"Nonsense." Mr. Jenkins waved a hand through the air. "You're like one of the family."

Elise approached, her eyes darting from Cash to Taryn. "Now I feel like I'm scaring you away." The woman's gaze settled on Taryn. "Please stay. I was hoping we could chat."

Taryn looked into Elise's warm green eyes. This family had a way of drawing her in.

"Okay."

Something wasn't right.

Cash had observed Taryn all night. And while she may have smiled and laughed with them over dinner and dominoes, there was a sadness in the depths of her blue eyes. Now, as they sat in the living room, he was still hard-pressed to figure out why.

"Well, I guess I've had enough excitement for today."

Gramps shoved out of his recliner, turned off the lamp on his side table and shuffled in the direction of his bedroom. "Good night, everyone."

"I'm right behind you, Dad." Cash's mom covered a yawn as she eased out of his grandma's recliner on the other side of the fireplace. "It's been a long day."

Taryn popped up off the couch. "I should be going."

"Don't be silly. You're much younger than we are. Take all the time you need." His mom gave her a hug. "I've enjoyed spending time with you." She stepped back, her gaze narrowing on Taryn. "And you've almost convinced me to try ice climbing." She held up a finger. "Almost."

Taryn grinned. "Just let me know when you're ready, Elise. I'll be happy to teach you."

His mother waved at him and started toward the stairs. "'Night, you two."

Cash reached for Taryn's hand and tugged her back down beside him. "Finally, I get to have you all to myself."

She blew out a soft laugh.

He flipped off the floor lamp beside him, leaving only the soft glow from the fireplace and the Tiffany lamp near the front window. He entwined their fingers as Scout snuggled between them. "Something's bothering you."

"What makes you say that?" She stared at the fire.

Laying a finger to her chin, he turned her head to face him. "I can see it in your eyes."

She let go a shaky breath. "My parents can't cosign the loan for me. It's not financially feasible for them." She glanced away now. "So, All Geared Up is no more. At least not for me."

"I'm sorry, Taryn." He stroked her cheek with the back of his hand. "I know how much this meant to you."

His heart ached for her. He knew all too well what it was like to have your dreams die. Yet, as much as he wanted to blurt out that he would give her the money, the words fell silent on the tip of his tongue. He'd prayed about it and God had yet to grant him peace.

"Yeah." A single tear rolled beneath his fingers. "But it's over." She pulled away, sniffed and swiped at the unwanted moisture. Fixed her gaze on the fire again. "So, now that your mom's here, when are you leaving?"

Leaving was the last thing he wanted to think about. But it was inevitable. He twisted toward her. "The week is half over, so I'm staying until Saturday."

She nodded, her expression hard. Resigned. Did that mean she didn't want him to leave?

"I was hoping that, with Mom here, maybe we could go ice climbing again."

Letting go of him, she shoved both her hands between her knees. Her shoulders stiffened. "I don't know. I'm pretty busy this week."

"Don't do this, Taryn."

"Do what?"

"Don't pull away from me. Try to act all tough. I know you don't want me to leave any more than I do."

"I'm a big girl. I'll get over it."

"I won't." He forced her to look at him again. "I'm falling in love with you, Taryn."

Her eyes closed. "Don't."

He inched closer, searching for the right words. "You know, maybe your not getting All Geared Up is a God thing."

She glared at him now.

"If you had bought the store, you'd be tied to Ouray, just like I'm tied to Dallas. But without it, you're free to do whatever you want." He took hold of her hand. "Like maybe come to Dallas. With me."

Her gaze searched his and, for a moment, he thought

she might say yes. Then her shoulders slumped and she shook her head. "I can't. I told you before, Cash, I'm never going back to Texas."

Chapter Sixteen

Cash couldn't be in love with her. And whatever he felt for her would be gone as soon as she told him everything.

Taryn took a deep breath and prayed for courage. The quicker she got through this, the better off they'd both be. "Things...happened while I was in Texas." She wiped her suddenly sweaty palms on her jeans. "Things I've kept hidden from almost everyone, including my family."

"What things?" He cupped her cheek, the caress of his thumb making it nearly impossible to think, let alone say what needed to be said.

Pulling away, she picked up Scout and hugged her to her chest. Shame and anguish washed over her as she stared at the orange-and-blue flames beyond the glass doors of the fireplace. "When I was a teenager, I could hardly wait to leave Ouray. I just knew I was made for bigger and better things than this little town. So I took my big ego and headed off to the University of North Texas, determined to have a career in television."

"Sounds like a typical teenager." Cash's voice held the hint of a smile.

She knew he was trying to keep things light, to make her feel better. But she had to keep going. No matter how much it hurt. "Shortly after I arrived, I met a guy. Brian. He was a junior, very suave, very charming." For the first time in a long while she allowed her mind to wander back to that day at the student union. "He said everything I wanted to hear. I fell hard and fast because he was exactly the kind of man I thought I wanted." Rich, charming... Recalling how she perpetually fed his ego, she wanted to puke.

Cash shifted beside her but didn't move away. Yet.

"Outside of class, we spent almost all of our time together, days and nights." Except those few weekends when Brian went home. She should have suspected something when he never asked her to join him.

"Right before Christmas break, he broke up with me. Told me I didn't fit into his plans." She kissed the top of Scout's head, drawing whatever strength she could from her tiny dynamo. "That was the worst Christmas ever." Most of it spent wondering what she'd done wrong and how she could make Brian love her again. Stupid.

She felt the warmth of Cash's hand as he rubbed her neck and shoulders. "Then I discovered I was pregnant."

The rubbing stopped. Only for a moment, but it wasn't the same. The strength, the tenderness his touch had held before was gone. Nothing would ever be the same between them.

"To add insult to injury, when I got back to school, I found out that Brian was engaged." She dared to look at Cash. "Apparently he had a girlfriend back home the entire time we were together." Despite the dim lighting, she could see the compassion in his eyes. And it nearly undid her.

He shook his head. "Did you tell him about the baby?"

She nodded, that old feeling of unworthiness intensifying. "He called me a liar. Said I was just using him for his money. Then he pulled out his wallet, handed me a wad of cash and told me to clean up my own mess." She had never felt so dirty. So...foolish.

Cash groaned and pulled her close. "Oh, Taryn. I am so sorry." She tried to pull away, but his hold tightened. "That jerk didn't deserve you."

In the circle of Cash's embrace, the tears came freely. "I was such a fool. I gave him everything I had, and it wasn't enough. *I* wasn't enough."

"Shh..." Cash held her while she buried her face in his chest and sobbed. For the innocence she lost then, for what her mistakes would cost her now. After a few minutes, she straightened and gathered her tattered emotions.

Scout wriggled free and settled between them once again.

Taryn stroked her wiry fur. "I went back to my dorm room, crawled into bed and stayed there. I didn't go to class, I didn't eat, I didn't sleep...and when the tears were gone, I felt like a hollow shell."

Her lips trembled into some semblance of a smile. "But I had a roommate who refused to give up on me. And despite how horribly I'd treated her during our first semester together, she took care of me. She sat with me, brought me food, hugged me, cried with me and prayed for me. It was because of her that I came to know Jesus."

Cash leaned forward, resting his forearms on his thighs, and looked at her with a sad smile.

"Suddenly I wasn't alone. But I wasn't prepared to be a mother." Half laughing, she shook her head. "And I certainly couldn't tell my parents."

His brow puckered in confusion. "Why not?"

"Are you kidding? Appearances are everything to my mother. If I had come back here pregnant, she would have disowned me."

He reached for her hand again. "Taryn, your mother may be annoying and you may not agree with everything she does, but she's not heartless. You don't really think she'd toss her own daughter aside."

Why had she brought up her parents? Cash obviously didn't know why her mother was so worried about appearances. Why she guarded her reputation at all costs.

Cash squeezed her hand. "So what did you do?"

"I went to an adoption center."

"What's that?"

"A home for unwed mothers." She stared at their entwined fingers. "I lived there while I was pregnant. Then I gave my baby up for adoption."

He blew out a long, slow breath. "I can't imagine how hard that must have been."

"It was the first unselfish thing I'd ever done in my life. But he was worth it."

"You had a son?"

She nodded. "David. He was beautiful." So tiny and perfect. She swiped away the tears that trailed down her cheeks and forced a smile. "But he has the most amazing mom and dad. A really neat Christian couple who weren't able to have a baby of their own." And she was blessed that they'd kept in touch with her all these years.

Cash tugged her toward him, but she resisted. "You are an extraordinary woman, Taryn Purcell."

"No, I'm not." She quickly stood and retrieved her coat from the post at the bottom of the stairs. "You need to go back to Dallas, Cash, and forget about me." She shoved her arms into the sleeves. "Because you deserve better."

"Taryn—" he was beside her in two strides "—come on. You don't mean that."

Determined, she bored her gaze into his. "Yeah, I do. Look, we've had a great time these past few weeks, and I'm glad I was able to remind you what it was like to have fun. But we're very different people. Things would never work out between us."

Arms folded across his chest, he looked hurt and confused. "If you think what you just told me will change my feelings for you, you're wrong."

"You say that now, but what about tomorrow or next week?" She felt the beanie in her pocket, yanked it out and put it on. "Once you've had time to process things, I'm sure you'll see that going our separate ways is for the best." She started for the door. "Scout?"

The dog hopped off the couch, stretched and ambled toward her.

"I know you're afraid of being hurt, but I'm not that guy, Taryn. I'm *not* Brian." Cash followed her. "I'm going to call you."

Why did he have to make this so difficult? All she wanted was to go home to her bed where she could cry without anyone ever knowing.

"I wish you wouldn't." Because it would break her heart every time they said goodbye, always wondering if that time would be the last. She reached for the knob and opened the door.

"Will you promise me one thing?"

She turned to look at him.

He closed the distance between them. "You need to tell your parents. They have a grandchild out there they don't even know about." He reached for her hand. "They love you. They'll understand."

Tears threatened again, but she managed to blink them away. "I can't promise you that, Cash." Any more than she could promise him anything else. "But I'll think about it." She gave his hand a final squeeze and walked out the door. "Goodbye, Cash."

Cash couldn't remember ever feeling so miserable. He and Yvette were together for two years and he barely missed a beat when she turned down his proposal. Sure, his pride took a hit, but his heart was still intact. The only thing that had ever come close was when he had to let go of his dream. Perhaps that's why this was so difficult. Taryn had become a part of a new dream.

Rolling over, he punched his pillow and stared at the taunting red numbers on the bedside clock: 6:00 a.m., and he had yet to get any sleep.

At least now he understood why Taryn refused to go back to Texas. But that was the only thing he understood, and it wasn't much of a consolation.

God, why won't she give me a chance? I get that that jerk Brian made her feel unworthy, but she's no longer that naive girl. She's a remarkable woman. The strength and courage she has is beyond my comprehension. Taryn deserves to be loved. To have a family. And I'd really like to be the guy to give her those things.

He wouldn't give up on her. He couldn't.

His cell phone vibrated on the nightstand. He grabbed it and looked at the screen. Dad. Probably wanting to know when he was coming back. Well, he'd just have to wait, because Cash intended to use these next few days to get through to Taryn.

"Hello."

"Morning, son." An actual greeting. Hmph. Maybe the old dog was capable of learning some new tricks, after all.

He rolled onto his back. Ran a hand through his hair. "Hey, Dad. Look, I'm not coming back until Saturday. I need a few—"

"I'm selling the company."

Cash couldn't have heard him right. "Excuse me?" He tossed the covers aside and rose to the side of the bed. "You're *what?*"

"Selling the company. I've had an offer from Chaparral and, frankly, it's too good to turn down."

"Chaparral? They're the largest trailer manufacturer in the U.S."

"I know. And they've got a good reputation."

This couldn't be happening. There's no way his father would sell Coble Trailers. Maybe he was trying to coerce Cash into coming back sooner. "But we've worked so hard to build Coble Trailers. You've given it your whole life. How could you just up and throw it all away?"

"I haven't accepted anything yet. I wanted to talk with you first."

He stood, grabbed his suitcase from the closet and tossed it on the bed. "Good. I'll be back in Dallas just as soon as I can. Don't do anything until I get there." Ending the call, he dropped the phone on the bed.

Unbelievable. This was totally out of character for his father. What would make him decide to sell now?

Who cares? You wouldn't be tied to Coble Trailers anymore.

True.

But he wouldn't have a job, either.

He quickly dressed before emptying the drawers and throwing whatever else he had laying around into the suitcase. What else was there? He was forgetting something. He rubbed his chin, the stubble rough against his fingers.

His shaving kit. He padded across the hardwood into the tiny hallway.

His mother emerged from the second of the two upstairs bedrooms. "What's all the noise?" She cinched the sash on her robe.

"I've got to get back to Dallas." He continued around her and retrieved his shaving kit from the bathroom. "Dad just called. You're not going to believe this." He stopped in the doorway and looked at his mother. "He says he's selling the company."

"I see." His mom nodded. "So he decided to accept the offer?"

"You knew about this?" No wonder she was so calm.

"We discussed it the other night, yes."

"And nobody felt the need to let me in on this little discussion." He pushed past her. "Good grief, Mom, I've poured my entire adult life into this company. I thought surely that would count for something."

"Cash…" His mother followed him into the bedroom. "I'm sure this was a very difficult decision for your father. But he's not getting any younger, you know. I worry about him." She pulled one of the wadded shirts from the suitcase and folded it. "Your father lives in a constant state of stress. I'm afraid he's going to have a stroke or a heart attack."

Cash had thought the same thing on more than one occasion. Still…

"But you should have seen him at Megan's this weekend. He was so smitten with the twins. And Annie Grace always brings out the best in him." She dropped the shirt and ran a hand across Cash's back. "I'd like to see him enjoy life for a change. You, too, for that matter."

Cash leaned into the comforting touch. "I get that, Mom." Some of Cash's fondest memories were the times they'd spent in Ouray as a family, when his dad would let go of work and focus on them. "I just wish he would have consulted me. This is my livelihood, too, you know."

"I know it is." The old iron bed creaked as she sat. "I heard you tossing and turning last night. Did something happen between you and Taryn?"

"I don't want to go into it right now." His focus needed to be on getting home.

His mom crossed her legs and looked up at him. "You really like her, don't you?"

"Yeah, I do." He closed the lid on his suitcase and zipped it.

"So do I." His mother stood and started out of the room. "I'll go make some coffee. That is, if your grandfather hasn't beaten me to it."

Fifteen minutes later, Cash said his goodbyes and loaded his suitcase in the backseat of his rented SUV. As he fired up the vehicle, he glanced at the house next door. There were no lights to indicate anyone was up. He hated to leave without telling Taryn, but he'd call her from the airport. Maybe, between now and then, he could figure out what to say.

At the intersection of Main and Fifth, he glanced left then right. A two- or more-hour drive over the passes or a forty-minute drive that was virtually a straight shot? No contest.

He took a right and headed toward Montrose. Even if he couldn't get a nonstop flight, he could potentially be on his way long before he'd even make it to Durango.

On his way out of town, he spotted All Geared Up. The noose around his heart tightened. How he wished he could help Taryn.

Shaking away the unwanted thought, he wound his way out of Ouray. What was his father thinking? Coble Trailers was supposed to be his legacy. Cash's legacy. What was Cash supposed to do if he sold?

He needed to talk to his father face-to-face. Chaparral must have offered a pretty sweet deal to have his father even contemplating walking away from the company. So, where did that leave Cash?

Years of hard work for nothing. His father didn't even want his opinion. Just once, he'd like his dad to treat him like a man. Someone he respected. Instead of the screwup his father still believed him to be.

Peering out over the awakening rangeland, he felt a

headache coming on. *Lord, everything was going so well. I don't get it. In less than twelve hours, everything I've ever wanted, ever worked for, is falling apart. Please, show me what I'm supposed to do.*

Thirty minutes later, he parked his rental car at the small regional airport and headed straight for the ticket counter. Luckily, there was a flight leaving in an hour and a half. Barring any problems with his connection out of Denver, he'd be in Dallas early this afternoon.

After closing out things with the rental agency and making it through security, he couldn't stand it anymore. He had to talk to Taryn. Yeah, it was still early, but she'd be up and he'd get to catch her before she left for work.

He reached into the breast pocket of his jacket.

No phone.

Odd. He remembered putting it there before he got into the car. Standing, he checked his jeans pockets then his carry-on but came up empty handed. Panic rose in his gut. He tried to mentally retrace his steps, but with no sleep, he definitely wasn't firing on all cylinders.

Could he have left it in the car? At Gramps's?

An announcement came over the intercom. His flight was about to board.

He rushed back to security. "Did y'all happen to find a cell phone?"

One agent checked with the next, all shaking their heads.

Cash walked away feeling completely helpless. Something he wasn't sure he'd ever felt before. And he didn't like it.

God, I don't know what You're up to, but I'm at Your mercy.

Chapter Seventeen

Taryn sat on the edge of her bed, staring at the picture of the eight-year-old boy with eyes so like hers. How could she tell her parents about David? What would they say? She expected her father to be accepting, but her mother? That was a different story.

Mom spent the first eighteen years of her life enduring the whispers of people in her small California town. Until her dad rescued her and brought her to Ouray. Now she was a respected member of the community. What would she do when she learned about Taryn's indiscretions? What would Taryn do if she rejected her?

Scout stretched beside her, then leaped off the bed, shook and looked at Taryn, tail wagging.

"You want to go downstairs, don't you?"

The dog cocked her head, her tail wagging faster.

Taryn stood and tucked the photos back into the envelope. As much as she hated to admit it, Cash was right. She needed to tell her folks, and had prayed all night that God would prepare them for what she was about to say.

Thoughts of Cash made her heart sink. The pain of last night was still fresh. But releasing Cash was the right thing to do. Soon enough he would realize that she wasn't the girl for him. And if they were still together, a guy as wonderful and chivalrous as him would carry on as if everything were okay, when he was suffocating inside.

Scout scampered between Taryn and the door.

"All right, baby. Let's get you outside." She followed Scout down the stairs and into the kitchen. As expected, her parents were both at the table.

"Morning, princess." Her father raised his coffee mug in salute.

"Did you and Cash have a good time last night?" Her mom added some honey to her oatmeal.

Taryn let Scout outside, the morning chill seeping into her bones. She rubbed her arms. Whatever she and Cash shared was now in the past. She needed to get over it and move on.

But a girl didn't just get over someone like Cash. Somehow, though, she would find a way to move on.

"I suppose." She headed for the coffeepot. "His mother came in yesterday."

"Oh, yeah?" Her mom dabbed a napkin at the corners of her mouth. "I'll have to make a point to get over and see Elise."

Taryn filled her mug and joined her parents at the table. "There's something I need to tell you guys." At their quick visual exchange, she held up a hand. "Don't worry, it has nothing to do with money." She took a deep breath. "Though that doesn't mean it's going to be easy."

"All right, now you're scaring me." Her mom reached across the table and laid a hand atop Taryn's.

"I'm not trying to scare you." Her gaze drifted from her mother to her father. "But I need to tell you about my time in Texas."

The lines between her dad's eyebrows grew deeper, and her mom looked as if she was about to cry as Taryn told them about Brian.

Her mom pressed a hand to her chest. "You were… pregnant?"

Taryn looked away, not wanting to see the reproach. "Yes."

"And you didn't tell us?" Despite his stern expression, her father's blue eyes shimmered.

"I couldn't."

His gaze never left her. "What do you mean you couldn't?"

"Because…well…because of the Barkers' daughter." She turned her eyes to her mother, who stared past her, her expression vacant. Did she even remember?

A sob, perhaps a gasp, escaped her mother. "I said I would disown her."

Taryn nodded, tears running down her cheeks.

"Everyone in town was talking about the Barkers' daughter." Her mom continued, "I remembered all those things people used to say about me and my mama because I was an illegitimate child. Oh, Taryn." Her mother practically tumbled her chair trying to get to her.

"I was afraid you wouldn't love me anymore." Taryn sobbed.

"You're my daughter. I could never stop loving you." Her mom clung to her as they cried. "I'm so sorry I said those things."

She didn't know how long they held on to each other. All Taryn knew was that she'd never felt more loved, accepted.

"What happened to the child?" Her father was still in his chair, a look of dread marring his handsome features.

Her mother eased into the chair beside her, still holding Taryn's hand.

Taryn sucked in a deep breath and straightened. "With or without your help, I wasn't ready to be a mother. So I gave him to this wonderful couple." She let go of her mom's hand and retrieved the envelope from her back pocket. She pulled out the photos the Hammonds had sent her over the years and laid them on the table, feeling as though she were baring her heart and soul for the first time. Probably because she was.

"His name is David." Tears spilled down her cheeks. She'd never shared these images with anyone, yet sharing them with her parents felt unbelievably right.

She hiccupped. "Can you ever forgive me?"

Her father knelt beside her and caressed her hair. "I don't think I've ever been more proud of you, princess." He kissed her cheek.

Scratching and whining sounded from the back door.

"Scout wants in." Taryn smiled at her father.

He patted her shoulder. "You sit tight." Her dad stood and crossed to the door.

Scout trotted right to her and stood on her hind legs, letting her cold paws rest on Taryn's thighs.

"Come here, baby." Taryn scooped her up and kissed her as Taryn's mom returned to her own chair. "I love you. Yes, I do." Taryn stroked the dog's head.

Her dad pulled his chair out and sat down. "You may not have been ready when David was born, but someday you'll make a great mom."

"Oh, I don't know about that." She absently rubbed Scout. "I don't think I'm cut out for marriage."

"What are you talking about?" Her mom shot her an incredulous look. "You have so much love to give."

"Yeah, but what man is going to want someone like me?" She shrugged. "I just don't feel...worthy."

"Taryn..." Her mom rounded the table again and sat down beside her. Took hold of her hands. "I spent half my life feeling inferior. Like I wasn't good for anything or anyone. But nothing is beyond redemption, honey. Not even my mama." The waterworks began again. "Before your grandmother died, I had the privilege of leading her to Jesus. So when she left this earth, she got to stand before Him perfect and blameless."

She cupped Taryn's chin. "Taryn Elizabeth, you are a child of God. That doesn't mean you're not going to make mistakes. But you are worthy of whatever blessings He sends your way."

An image of Cash popped into her mind. He was definitely a blessing. But could he really look beyond her mistakes? He said it wouldn't change his feelings for her. But that was last night. Things often look different in the light of day.

I'm falling in love with you.

"And I'm thinking that young man next door may be one of them." Reaching across the table, her mother grabbed her mug from the table and stood. "Anyone else need their coffee warmed?"

Could Mom be right? Taryn thought maybe God had brought them together for her to help Cash. But could it be the other way around?

Nervous excitement bubbled in the pit of her stomach. She had to talk to him.

Bolting from her chair, she grabbed her jacket and shoved her feet into her boots. "I'll be right back. I've got to talk to Cash."

She hurried out the door, jogging across the snowy yard and up Mr. Jenkins's front steps. Her heart was pounding as she knocked.

Elise smiled when she opened the door. "Good morning, Taryn."

"Is Cash around?"

Elise's smile faded. "He didn't call you?"

"No, I haven't talked to him since last night."

"Oh." Elise looked distressed. "I'm sorry, Taryn. Cash went back to Dallas today."

Her heart dropped to her feet. "O-okay." She turned,

realizing Cash's rental was no longer parked in front of the house. "Um, well, maybe he'll call later." She waved. "Thank you."

She hurried back home just as quick as she came, only this time embarrassment propelled her steps. Cash would not call later, of that she was sure. After all, she'd told him to forget about her. That things would never work out. Once he'd had time to think, he obviously realized how right she was.

Though a part of her wished he'd proved her wrong.

She blew through the back door of her parents' house, struggling for air.

"That was quick." Her mother stood beside her dad, holding the most recent picture of David.

Taryn grabbed hold of one of the straight-back chairs, feeling as though her world had imploded.

"Honey, what's wrong?" Her mom left the picture with her dad and hurried to Taryn's side.

"He's gone." Her grip tightened for fear she might fall over.

"Cash?"

She nodded, blinking back tears.

"Well, I'm sure he'll be back."

"No. He went back to Dallas." Taryn pulled the chair out and collapsed into it. "He didn't even say goodbye." A sob caught in her throat, but she swallowed it away. She didn't want to cry. Didn't like to cry. And, until recently, never cried.

Her mom knelt beside her, holding her hands. "That doesn't sound like Cash. Maybe something happened."

"Yeah. I told him about my past."

"Taryn—" her dad came up behind her and laid a hand on her shoulder "—we all have pasts. You're not the same person you were back then. Any man worth his salt is going to know that."

As much as she wanted to believe her father, evidence to the contrary was too overwhelming.

A knock sounded at the back door and Scout started barking.

Taryn shushed the dog and scooped her up as her dad opened the door.

"Elise? What a nice surprise." He stepped back to allow Cash's mother to enter.

"Good to see you, Phil." She turned to Taryn's mother. "Bonnie." Her gaze fell to Taryn. "Mind if we talk?"

Taryn set Scout to the floor, stood and shrugged out of her jacket. "Okay."

"Can I get you some coffee?" Her mom was halfway across the kitchen.

"Coffee would be great, thank you." Elise took off her coat but left the beautiful aquamarine scarf draped around her neck.

Her dad hung the coat on a hook by the door. "Sorry I can't hang around. I need to get to work." He grabbed his own jacket.

Taryn helped him put it on then gave him a hug. "Thanks, Dad. For everything."

He kissed the top of her head. "I love you, princess."

As her father headed out the door, Taryn poured herself a fresh cup before joining her mother and Elise at the table. Heat seeped through the ceramic, warming her frozen fingers.

"I wanted to apologize to you, Taryn." Elise wrapped her long fingers around her mug. "You were gone before I thought to explain why Cash left in such a hurry."

"You don't owe me any explanation, Elise."

She patted Taryn's free hand. "Sweetie, I saw the look on your face."

Was it that obvious? Taryn glanced over at the corner. Scout had curled up in her bed.

"Cash got some upsetting news from his father early this morning regarding the company. Within an hour he was packed and on his way to the airport."

"I see." But she still couldn't help wondering if he would have left so abruptly had he not known about her past.

"Is everything all right?" Her mother regarded Elise.

"It will be. Cash and his father just have some things they need to work out." Elise turned her attention back to Taryn. "You know, my son is very taken with you."

"He's a good friend." If they were even that anymore.

"Oh, don't kid yourself, Taryn. I've seen the two of you together. There's more than just friendship." Cash's mother lifted her cup. "Especially where Cash is concerned. I don't think there was a phone call I shared with him that he didn't talk about you." She took a sip. "You made my son smile again."

Taryn cradled her mug. "He's a workaholic. I just helped him loosen up a bit."

"You did much more than that."

Her gaze inadvertently drifted to Elise.

"You brought him back to life. Cash hasn't been this happy in ages."

"I think being away from Dallas had a lot to do with it."

"Perhaps. But that doesn't account for the gleam in his eye whenever he talks about you or looks at you. I know Cash is very fond of you."

Taryn pushed her chair away from the table and stood. "I appreciate you trying to make me feel better, Elise, but you couldn't possibly know what Cash is feeling for me."

"Of course I could. He told me himself just this morning."

Halfway to the coffeepot, Taryn froze. Turned back to Elise. "What else did he say?"

Cash's mother sighed. "Not much, I'm afraid. I asked him if something happened between the two of you after I went to bed last night, but he refused to talk about it. Whatever it was, though, kept him awake all night."

Taryn slumped back into her chair. "He wasn't the only one." But why was Cash tossing and turning? Because he still wanted to be with her even though she'd given him the brush-off? Or because the truth was too much to bear?

She shook her head. "I don't even know why we're having this conversation. Cash is gone. End of story."

"Honey, this story is far from over." Her mother chuckled.

Elise cocked her head. "Taryn, how do you feel about Cash?"

"Like I said, we're fr—"

"She loves him."

Taryn glared at her mother.

"You can try to deny it all you want, young lady, but I've seen the way you look at him." Her mother wagged a finger. "You get that same gleam Elise mentioned whenever you so much as think about Cash."

Taryn's cheeks heated. She did love Cash. So very much.

I'm falling in love with you.

Question was, did he still feel the same way?

She set her cup on the table and tried to wrap her brain around the possibility.

"Regardless of what we may or may not feel for each other, Cash is gone. He hasn't called or texted—"

"Go after him."

She shot Cash's mother an incredulous look. "What?"

Elise leaned closer. "Go after him."

"Um, no, I don't think so. Don't you watch romance

movies, Elise? It's the hero who goes after the girl, not the other way around."

"But it's Cash who needs to be rescued." She reached for Taryn. "And you, my dear, are the heroine in this saga."

She glanced at her mother, hoping she would offer her a way out.

Her mom's brows arched. "You are part of the rescue team, honey. Who knows? This could be your best rescue yet."

Taryn dropped her head in her hands. "No. This is crazy." She looked up. "What if he rejects me? What if he doesn't want me to come after him?"

"Well, then we'll cross that bridge when we come to it." Elise winked at Taryn's mother. "But I don't think that's going to happen."

"And if you don't," said her mom. "You'll always wonder what if."

Frustration nipped at Cash's heels as he barreled into the lobby of Coble Trailers. No phone. No Taryn. And, if his father had his way, no business. This day couldn't possibly get any worse.

He stormed through the showroom, past trailer displays.

"Cash? I wasn't expecting you." His assistant jumped to her feet, her high heels clicking on the marble floor, and followed him into his office.

"Where's my father?" He dropped his computer bag into the first of two leather guest chairs.

"Probably out in the shop. Do you want me to get him?"

Rubbing the back of his neck, he faced the tall brunette who had been with him a little over two years. "Yes, Jackie. Tell him to meet me in his office."

While she scurried off, he stopped by the restroom to splash some cool water on his face. Gripping the sides of the sink, he caught a glimpse of himself in the mirror.

Dark circles rimmed his eyes and stubble shadowed his chin. He was a mess.

Lord, I need Your help. I don't want this to be about me. Show me what You would have me do.

He wandered down the hall, into his father's office. An artist's rendering of their new building hung prominently on the wall, while family photos lined the knotty-pine bookshelves and credenza. Pausing at the first bookshelf, he scanned the pictures, his gaze stopping on the bottom shelf. He stooped to pick up the frame.

"I remember this." He stared at the image of him and his father holding up a stringer of trout. He must have been about eight. The whole family had gone to Ouray that year and he and his dad went fishing. Cash remembered how good it felt to be in Ouray and to have his dad pay attention to him instead of work.

"Welcome back, son."

Cash startled at his father's voice. He replaced the old photograph. "About time you got here."

Warren Coble stood in the doorway, hands perched on his hips. "I could say the same thing." He relaxed then and continued into the room. "Have a seat, Cash."

Cash closed the door before sitting in one of the two leather wingback chairs facing the desk. "So what gives? You've been nagging me to get back here for weeks and suddenly you've decided to sell the company. What is this, some manipulation tactic so you can finally get your way?"

The man leaned back in his leather desk chair and steepled his fingers. "If it were, I'd say it worked just fine."

After a momentary stare down, his father leaned forward and rested his arms on the massive desk. "But it wasn't. This offer from Chaparral came out of the blue."

"When?"

"End of last week."

Cash narrowed his gaze. "And you never mentioned it?"

"Son, I wasn't even entertaining their offer until your mother talked me into visiting Megan and her family this past weekend."

He crossed one leg over the other. "So what changed your mind?"

"Honestly? I had fun." His father chuckled and leaned back. "I didn't think I even knew how to relax anymore. But I did. And, by golly, it felt good."

Cash smiled. He could certainly relate. And if it hadn't been for Taryn, he'd still be every bit as wound up as he was when he first arrived in Ouray.

"I'm tired, Cash." His father's countenance changed. Not agitated or uptight the way he usually was, just serious. Honest. "I don't know how much longer the good Lord intends to keep me on this earth, but I'd like to enjoy it while I can."

"I can appreciate that, Dad. Really. But I feel as though you're just selling the company right out from under me. From the time you got sick, I've put my heart and soul into this business."

"And I appreciate that more than you'll ever know." His father stood, rounded the desk and settled in the chair beside Cash. "Son, this company was my dream. And you've built it into something bigger than I ever could have imagined. Which is why I plan to give you half of what Chaparral is offering." He leaned forward, resting his arms on his thighs. "But this was never your dream."

"How do you know that, Dad? When was the last time you asked me what I wanted?"

His father's steel-blue eyes shimmered. "I robbed you of your dreams, Cash. And for that, I am truly sorry. I had no right."

Guilt wound its icy grip around Cash's heart. "But

if you hadn't, who would have run things when you got sick?"

His dad gave him a sad smile. "Cash, if you can look me in the eye and tell me that you want Coble Trailers, I'll hand it to you lock, stock and barrel."

He studied his father. "And what about you?"

"I'll walk clean away. Besides, I'm sure your mother will have enough things to keep me busy for a few years."

Coble Trailers had consumed Cash's every thought for the last ten years. And how many times had he wished he could run things without his father breathing down his neck? Being sole owner, he'd finally be free to implement some of his ideas, instead of being at the beck and call to his father's whims.

An image of Taryn flashed through his mind. That first day when she took him climbing. The pain in her eyes when she left him last night. Man, he missed her. He wished he could talk this over with her. Wished he could talk to her, period.

"What do you say, Cash? What do *you* want?"

What did he want? Closing his eyes, he leaned against the soft leather of the chair. All he could think of was Ouray. God's splendor and majesty on full display. Taryn. The invigoration of conquering a slab of ice. The sense of community. All Geared Up.

It all felt so right.

His eyes popped open. He straightened. "I want to move to Ouray, buy All Geared Up and beg Taryn Purcell to be my wife."

His father lifted a brow. "What's All Geared Up?"

"It's a store that caters to outdoor enthusiasts."

"And Taryn is the young lady who's made you smile again?"

Cash couldn't help grinning. "Yes, she is."

His father held out his hand. "I'm proud of you, son. I halfway expected you'd do what you thought I wanted you to do. But you followed your heart. Well done."

If Cash hadn't been sitting down, he would have fallen over. He'd been striving for his father's approval all his life. And he'd finally achieved it. Not by doing what his father wanted, but by doing what *he* wanted. Tears blurred his vision as he reached for his father's hand.

His dad pulled him in for a huge bear hug. "I know I haven't said it near enough, but I love you, son."

"I love you too, Dad."

His father released him. "Guess I ought to call that fella over at Chaparral." He stood. "And you should go ahead and make an offer on that All Geared Up place. That is, unless you want to call Taryn first."

"I wish I could." He rose to stand eye to eye with his father. "I lost my phone this morning, so I don't have her number."

"Well, somebody's bound to have it. Start making some phone calls, boy." His dad popped him on the shoulder.

Cash laughed as he exited his father's office. Incredible. He didn't know if he'd ever seen his father like this. *Lord, You are truly a miracle worker. Thank You.*

"Mr. Coble?" The receptionist caught him in the hallway. "There's someone here to see you."

Whoever it was, he'd have to get rid of them. He couldn't focus on work if he wanted to.

"Thank you, Stacy." Rounding the corner into the showroom, he was certain his lack of sleep had his mind playing tricks on him, because he thought he saw Taryn sitting in one of their reception chairs.

He blinked twice and both times she was still there.

She stood and met him halfway, her high-heeled boots

clicking against the marble floor. And that dress. Wow. Right now she looked far more Dallas than Ouray.

His gaze drifted from the dress to her golden-brown hair and those eyes he loved so much. "What are you doing here?" He couldn't stop looking at her. He wanted to memorize every nuance.

Her smile was definitely nervous. "I love you. And, if you're still interested in pursuing this—" she waved a hand between them "—thing between us, I'm willing to give Dallas a try."

Cash thought his heart might explode in his chest. Forget this day getting worse. It just kept getting better and better. "No. You can't stay in Dallas."

Her smile dissipated and she lowered her head.

"Because I'm moving to Ouray."

Her beautiful head popped back up, her eyes sparkling like fine gemstones. "You're moving to Ouray?"

"Yep." He took a step closer. "And I plan on buying All Geared Up."

She blinked several times, her hand covering her mouth.

"If it's all right with you."

She nodded. "I can't think of anyone better."

He slipped an arm around her waist and tugged her closer. "Of course, I'm going to need a partner. Preferably someone who knows what outdoor enthusiasts want."

She slid her hands over his shoulders and around his neck. "I might be able to think of someone."

Gazing down at Taryn, he couldn't remember when he'd been happier. "It'll be a long-term commitment."

She cocked her head, a smile tipping the corners of her mouth. "How long did you have in mind?"

"How about forever?"

Unshed moisture glistened in her unfaltering gaze. "Sounds good to me."

"I love you, Taryn." Eliminating whatever distance remained between them, he lowered his head and kissed her.

The woman he'd always dreamed of, yet never imagined he would ever find, melted against him. She'd rescued him from himself, showing him what it was like to truly live. And he planned to spend a lifetime making all her dreams come true.

Epilogue

In only two short—or perhaps long—weeks, Taryn would be Mrs. Cash Coble.

Looking around the home Cash had bought for them, the one he'd spent all summer renovating, her heart swelled with joy.

"For a bridal shower, that wasn't half-bad."

Taryn eyed her intended as he snatched another carrot from the table in their new dining room. "It wasn't a bridal shower, Cash. It was a housewarming party. Right, Blakely?"

"Nope." Trent picked up a miniature cheesecake. "It was a shower."

"And what makes you say that?" Blakely's gaze narrowed on her husband.

"Look at all this stuff." Trent gestured to the spread of gifts in the adjoining living room. "It's all for girls. Cash, did you see one power tool in the whole lot?"

He shook his head. "Not a one."

Taryn sidled up beside him, admiring the stunning engagement ring he'd presented her with at the top of Mount Sneffels. A beautiful round solitaire with more diamonds trailing down each side of the band. "What about that bright red stand mixer my parents gave us? That's got lots of power."

He tugged her against him. "Not quite what I had in mind, though, darlin'." With that glimmer in his eye, darlin' had become her favorite endearment.

"Oh, you've got tons of power tools." Tools he had already put to good use restoring the old craftsman-style house. "Me, on the other hand—" she wandered toward the newly remodeled kitchen "—this is my very first kitchen ever. I need all this stuff so I can cook for you."

Blakely laughed. "Girl, we may never get you out of there. I bet Cash gains ten pounds your first month of marriage."

"If not more." He shook his head. "I can only imagine what the holidays are going to be like."

"Ooo…" Taryn rubbed her hands in anticipation. "I can hardly wait."

"First things first." Cash reeled her in once again. "We still have to get this wedding out of the way."

Staring up at that face she loved so much, she knew October 1 couldn't arrive soon enough for her. But with the spring purchase of All Geared Up, followed by some remodeling and the high season, a fall wedding was their best option.

Besides, that gave Cash's grandfather plenty of time to recover. Now they couldn't keep the old man down. He'd even pitched in to help with some of the projects at the store and the house. Just nothing that involved ladders.

"Yes. And preferably while I can still fit into my matron-of-honor dress." Blakely smoothed a hand over her ever-expanding belly.

Trent smiled, laying a hand atop his wife's. "I've never seen a more beautiful baby bump."

Watching the exchange, Taryn smiled. She couldn't

be happier for her friend. Her gaze inadvertently drifted to Cash.

Wearing a mischievous grin, he ambled alongside her. "I bet you'd look mighty fine with one of those."

Heat rushed to her cheeks. "Easy, cowboy."

"Knock, knock." Taryn's mother poked her head in the front door.

Scout barked and darted for the door, tail wagging.

Her parents couldn't have been gone more than thirty minutes. She wondered why they were back so soon.

"Come on in, Mom." Approaching the door, she saw Elise was with her. "What's going on?"

"We come bearing gifts." Her father grunted under the weight of whatever the cloth-covered item was that he and Warren were carrying up the steps.

"Y'all need some help?" Cash held the door wide.

His dad smiled. "We're good, son."

"What do you mean, gifts?" Taryn eyed her mother. "You've already given us so much." Aside from the mixer, they were paying for her entire wedding.

"These are special gifts," her mother pointed out with a wink.

Scout skittered out of the way as the men settled the piece on the hardwood floor in the living room.

Trent and Blakely gathered with them.

Tears in her eyes, her mom stood beside the draped object, her gaze trained on Taryn. "Honey, you know how much I love refurbishing things. Which is why I'm so glad you two bought this magnificent old house."

Everyone nodded in agreement.

"Cash, you've done a wonderful job in here," she continued.

He smiled and nodded, his arm around Taryn's waist. "Thank you, Bonnie."

"However—" she held up a finger "—Elise and I decided it needed something else."

Taryn glanced up at Cash, who was wearing the same confused look.

Cash's mother took a step forward. "Something that unites our two families." She grinned at Taryn's mom.

"So…" Mom tugged off the covering.

"Oh, my." Chill bumps erupted down Taryn's arms as she took in the oddly familiar piece. "Is that your hutch?"

"The very one."

"Wow." Cash smoothed a hand over the satin finish. "This is some of the prettiest oak I've ever seen."

"Taryn, do you remember when I first brought this home?"

"Yeah. It was the ugliest, most decrepit thing I'd ever seen."

Everyone laughed.

"Pretty banged up, too. Lots of scrapes and scars." Her mother approached and took her hand. "Not so unlike us."

Taryn blinked back the tears that threatened.

"So that got me to thinking." Her mom scanned the faces of those gathered round. "One day I decided to strip off that red paint I'd added. And you know what I discovered?" Her gaze stopped on Taryn.

"What?"

"All those scrapes and scars I'd tried to cover up only added to the beauty of the natural wood."

Taryn blinked faster. "It's gorgeous, Mom. But it's yours."

"Not anymore. I want you to have it, honey. As a reminder of how beautiful you are, flaws and all." Her mother embraced her, and the tears Taryn had been battling finally won out.

Her mom let go, wiping her own cheeks. "Your turn, Elise."

Cash's mother smiled, her gaze flitting between Cash and Taryn. "A piece as special as this one needs to be filled with something equally important. So…" She held out a medium-size gift bag.

"Thanks, Mom." Cash took the bag and handed it to Taryn.

She rummaged through the white tissue paper and pulled out a dessert plate. Her gaze went to Elise. "Your mother's china." She fingered the turquoise border, the scalloped edges and the delicate pink flowers, remembering the day she and Elise found the box in Mr. Jenkins's attic.

"The rest of it is in the truck. It's yours now."

Taryn's mouth dropped open. "Are you sure? What about Megan?"

"Taryn, I saw the awe and reverence in your eyes when we found this set. These dishes deserve to be appreciated again."

"Thank you." She hugged her soon-to-be mother-in-law.

"Our past is a part of us, Taryn. We shouldn't hide it away." Elise released her, held her at arm's length. "God wants us to use it to serve others."

Elise was right. Taryn's past was a part of her, made her who she was today. Once she accepted that, she was free. Free to love. Free to be loved.

"Thank you all so much." Hugging the plate to her chest, she slipped an arm around Cash and looked from Elise to Warren to her mom and dad. "I will cherish these always."

Cash tipped her chin to look at him and she saw her own appreciation reflected in his eyes. "And I will cherish you." He stroked her hair. "Because just like our moms rescued these incredible pieces, you rescued me." Then he pressed his lips to hers.

Tucked in the haven of Cash's embrace, Taryn's past, present and future surrounded her. God was so good. Now she could hardly wait to be Cash's wife and fill this once forgotten house with children. Because, like her mother said, nothing is beyond redemption.

* * * * *

Dear Reader,

Have you ever watched a dream die? Cash and Taryn both experienced the death of a dream, only to have God restore those dreams in ways they never could have imagined. God knows our hearts, yet He usually doesn't do things the way we think He should. Instead, He does something far beyond our expectations, but He does it in His perfect time.

From the moment Taryn appeared on the pages of *The Doctor's Family Reunion,* I knew I had to tell her story. It takes a strong woman, with a tremendous amount of love, to give a baby up for adoption. Like Hannah, the mother of Samuel, in the Bible. Hannah was barren and longed for a child. Yet after praying to God to give her a son, she gave the boy over to the Lord through Eli the priest. Then she praised God for restoring her dream, saying, "The Lord brings death and makes alive."

I hope you enjoyed *Rescuing the Texan's Heart* and revisiting the charming town of Ouray. Located in southwestern Colorado, Ouray is known by many names—the Switzerland of America, the Gem of the Rockies, the Ice Climbing Capital of the United States, and the Jeeping Capital of the World. And it's one of my favorite places in the world.

I love to connect with my readers. You can contact me via my website, www.mindyobenhaus.com or you can snail mail me c/o Love Inspired Books, 233 Broadway, Suite 1001, New York, NY 10279.

Hoping all your dreams come true,
Mindy

Questions for Discussion

1. Cash was just being himself when he called Taryn "darlin'," but the combination of that word and his Texas drawl made it difficult for Taryn to see him for who he really was. Have you ever cast judgment on someone without getting to know them first?

2. Cash was a workaholic. Are you, or have you ever known, anyone who's a workaholic? Were they happy or stressed? How did this affect their relationship with family/friends?

3. Many people questioned Taryn's desire to purchase All Geared Up because she'd have to give up being a guide. Have you ever made a decision that those close to you questioned? Have you ever had to give up something you loved to do to achieve another goal?

4. Cash used his injured knee as an excuse when Taryn brought up the subject of ice climbing. Yet, she wasn't afraid to push him out of his comfort zone. Have you ever known anyone who wasn't afraid to challenge people?

5. When Cash witnessed the car crash on the mountain, he risked his own safety to help the victims. How do you think you would react if you found yourself in a similar situation?

6. Taryn feared telling her mother about the baby she had because, as a child, she'd heard her mother claim she would disown her. Have you ever said some-

thing you didn't mean only to have it come back and haunt you?

7. Cash blamed himself for his grandfather's accident because he'd failed to cut the tree limb like he'd promised. Have you ever blamed yourself for something that happened because of something you did or didn't do?

8. Taryn spent a lot of years trying to hide her past, but ultimately learned that her past made her the person she is today. Have you ever tried to hide something from your past? How did hiding it affect you?

9. Cash put work above everything, including his relationship with God. Have you ever been so busy with other things that you've squeezed God out of your life without realizing it?

10. When Taryn's loan was denied, she felt her world was imploding. Has there ever been an event in your life that's made you feel your world was crumbling? How did you react?

11. Taryn gave up her child because she knew she wasn't ready to be a mother. Have you ever sacrificed something you deeply loved because you knew it was the right thing to do?

REQUEST YOUR FREE BOOKS!

2 FREE INSPIRATIONAL NOVELS
PLUS 2
FREE
MYSTERY GIFTS

Love Inspired

YES! Please send me 2 FREE Love Inspired® novels and my 2 FREE mystery gifts (gifts are worth about $10). After receiving them, if I don't wish to receive any more books, I can return the shipping statement marked "cancel." If I don't cancel, I will receive 6 brand-new novels every month and be billed just $4.74 per book in the U.S. or $5.24 per book in Canada. That's a saving of at least 21% off the cover price. It's quite a bargain! Shipping and handling is just 50¢ per book in the U.S. and 75¢ per book in Canada.* I understand that accepting the 2 free books and gifts places me under no obligation to buy anything. I can always return a shipment and cancel at any time. Even if I never buy another book, the two free books and gifts are mine to keep forever.

105/305 IDN F47Y

Name _____ (PLEASE PRINT)

Address _____ Apt. #

City _____ State/Prov. _____ Zip/Postal Code

Signature (if under 18, a parent or guardian must sign)

Mail to the **Harlequin® Reader Service:**
IN U.S.A.: P.O. Box 1867, Buffalo, NY 14240-1867
IN CANADA: P.O. Box 609, Fort Erie, Ontario L2A 5X3

Are you a subscriber to Love Inspired books
and want to receive the larger-print edition?
Call 1-800-873-8635 or visit www.ReaderService.com.

* Terms and prices subject to change without notice. Prices do not include applicable taxes. Sales tax applicable in N.Y. Canadian residents will be charged applicable taxes. Offer not valid in Quebec. This offer is limited to one order per household. Not valid for current subscribers to Love Inspired books. All orders subject to credit approval. Credit or debit balances in a customer's account(s) may be offset by any other outstanding balance owed by or to the customer. Please allow 4 to 6 weeks for delivery. Offer available while quantities last.

Your Privacy—The Harlequin® Reader Service is committed to protecting your privacy. Our Privacy Policy is available online at www.ReaderService.com or upon request from the Harlequin Reader Service.

We make a portion of our mailing list available to reputable third parties that offer products we believe may interest you. If you prefer that we not exchange your name with third parties, or if you wish to clarify or modify your communication preferences, please visit us at www.ReaderService.com/consumerchoice or write to us at Harlequin Reader Service Preference Service, P.O. Box 9062, Buffalo, NY 14269. Include your complete name and address.

LI13R

Hunter Jacobson wants no part of his grandfather's matchmaking. The lone cowboy is certain that's what the old man is doing when he trades part of their Montana ranch for Scarlett Murphy's shares of an old Alaska gold mine. Or is he running one of his legendary scams on the sweet single mom? A trip to Dry Creek, Alaska, reveals the truth—and brings Hunter and Scarlett face-to-face with a past family feud and a vulnerable present. But surprisingly it's the future that intrigues Hunter most…if he can get Scarlett to make him her groom.

◆ NORTH *to* DRY CREEK ◆

The road to Alaska is paved with love

Alaskan Sweethearts

by

Janet Tronstad

Available October 2014
wherever Love Inspired books
and ebooks are sold.

LI87914